NIGHTMAN

NIGHTMAN

a novel

by

James Pendleton and Jerome Johnson

ISBN 1-883911-61-3

Library of Congress Control Number: 2004095325

Brandylane Publishers, Inc.
Richmond, Virginia
www.brandylanepublishers.com

1

Call me the night man. That's what I am mostly.
Course, I work some in the daytime too, cleaning houses for
my special customers—nice folks who live in a pretty part of
town. But mainly I work at night. That's when most of the
people in my trade get busy. After the rest of you folks go
home for the day, we come out to clean up the mess.

Office buildings, car dealerships, churches, schools,
karate clubs, and places like the Sharon Clinic for Women.
I've got keys to more offices and homes in this town than I
can count. Lots of keys. But most of 'em to office buildings.
People come to work in the morning and find their offices all
shiny—windows cleaned, trash cans emptied, books dusted,
yesterday's soda cans hauled away, rugs vacuumed, and, oh
yes, the occasional wrapper from a hurriedly opened con-
dom scooped up neatly from underneath a desk. Like magic.
I guess it makes people feel like no matter what they do,
there's always somebody to make things right by morning.

Now you might think my job is dull, day after day,
night after night, cleanin' up other people's trash. But lately
I've started thinking of my work as entertainment. Really.
It's kind of like what an off duty airline pilot once told me

when I asked him what it was like to fly, and he said, "Well, it's made up of long periods of boredom sandwiched in between slices of pure terror and excitement." And I've had all of 'em in my time. You never know what you're gonna find when you park your pickup in a dark alley and go into what's supposed to be an empty office building late at night. Just last month I went to work as usual at the Corporation Headquarters about ten o'clock one night. (I'm not gonna tell you the name of this corporation just like I'm not gonna tell you the real names of anybody in this story, because if I did, somebody would be planting a bomb under my truck by the end of the week.) But anyway, I went into the building, and I found this guy, young guy, maybe seventeen or eighteen, walkin' down the hall when I come out the elevator on the second floor. Now I was just bringin' my cleaning stuff·into the building, and all I had with me were my mops and my bucket. So I said to him, knowin' that the building was supposed to be empty, I said, "Can I help you?" Just as polite as could be, you understand, 'cause you never know what you're dealin' with in situations like that, and I could already tell by the time he was within ten feet of me that he was on somethin'. You know, big dilated pupils and a far off dreamy look in his eyes.

And he said, sort of slurred, you know, "I'm lookin' for Mr. Phillips' office."

Of course, I knew there won't nobody named Phillips in the building, but I didn't tell him, 'cause I didn't want to argue with him. So I said, "I don't know Mr. Phillips, but if you'll come downstairs with me, I'll show you the directory and we can look him up. And he did it."

We looked at the directory on the wall by the front door, where of course, there was no 'Mr. Phillips.' "I'll tell you what," I said. "He ain't in the directory, but if you'll come back during regular business hours between 9:00 and 5:00, I'm sure the receptionist will help you. But right now the building is closed."

And he said, "OK" and turned and went out the door that I was already holdin' open for him.

That was one of the easier ones. But thinking about it later and wondering how and when he got into the building made me mark it as the time when things really began to go a little crazy in this town. Now, in case you don't remember, let me remind you that for the last few years our home town of Richmond, Virginia, has been ranked by the FBI among the five top murder capitals of the United States, right up there next to New Orleans and Detroit which are much larger cities. People like to think New York is a big crime city, but New York is a peaceful garden compared to the shooting galleries that operate along Richmond's back streets. So you can see why I get a little nervous when things start to get out of line.

Sometimes, I think that Richmond has never got over being burned down at the end of the Civil War. Half the population was made up of newly freed slaves who didn't know where to go or what to do, and half the population was made of newly defeated white people who had lost their property, and everybody was mad as hell. That sort of feeling don't just go away when things start to change, no matter how polite people learn to be. It gets passed down some way or other, and when you mix it with the drug trade that hit this city in the 80s and 90s, it's like gunpowder and gasoline. So keep this in mind when I talk about Richmond after dark.

Now, the day after I found the young guy at the Corporation was a pretty quiet day for me, except that I changed my routine slightly. I cleaned a couple of private homes during the afternoon, but since Wednesday night was a night that the Sharon Clinic stayed open late, I went by the Corporation Headquarters first to catch them early in the evening. Things seemed quiet when I got there just at dark. Building locked. No strangers wanderin' through the halls. So I went about doin' what I usually do, and on that night, I started at the top with Mr. Shields's office. Now, Mr. Shields is the head of the Corporation, CEO, I guess you'd call him, and he is some big muckity muck in this town. I mean, listen. In addition to his job at the Corporation, Mr. Shields is on the board of near'bout every big outfit you can name, Crestar Bank, Commonwealth University, the Virginia Electric and Power Company, the Museum. And of course, he's on the vestry of the same Episcopal church where General Robert E. Lee—Ol' Marse Robert, himself—went to church. I mean, you can bet that when the president of the university wants to make changes, he consults Mr. Shields for advice, and when the Governor wants to talk to somebody about economic policy, he also consults Mr. Shields for advice.

And the Museum, forget it. Nobody at the Museum will even sneeze without consulting Mr. Shields (or his wife), but that's a story I'll get to later on. He's even a major stock holder in the Sharon Clinic for Women, where I also work almost every night of the week. So you can see that bein' on Mr. Shields's good side can make you feel like you're going somewhere.

Anyway, on that day, I unlocked the door to the outer office—this was right about 6:30, I guess—and started emptyin' trash cans into my bag before I would turn on the vacuum cleaner. And then, all of a sudden I got the feelin' that somethin' was different. I don't know what it was. Don't know whether I heard somethin' or smelled somethin'. Don't know what. But I had the feelin' I wasn't alone. So I looked in the coat closet and under the secretary's desk, and then I headed for Mr. Shields' inner office. I pulled out my key, stuck it in the lock, turned the knob, and—what a surprise!

It is very difficult to describe adequately just how silly a man looks with his britches down around his ankles. But that's what I saw when I opened that door—Mr. Shields with his britches down. His back was to me but I knew it was him, and he was standin' there facing his desk with his britches around his ankles and his white ass shinin' like the rising sun in my direction, and sitting on the desk in front of him—facing him—was Miss Blowzer, Janet Blowzer, I think is her name, the pretty secretary he'd hired to assist Mrs. Wellford, his regular secretary, about six months before. She had her legs around his waist, and she had one shoe on and one shoe off and her panties hangin' over one ankle, and she was lookin' directly at me across his shoulder when I opened the door. "Oh My God! Braxton!" she yelled, screamin' like she was bein' stuck with somethin' a lot more painful than what Mr. Shields was stickin' her with. "Braxton, get out of here. Get out!"—shoutin' at me like I was a dog or sump'n.

And I just said, "Excuse me," and closed the door and backed all the way out of the office into the hall as fast as I could.

Now understand that this is inherently a very dangerous situation. Just on the face of it, realize that more than one man has been shot in this town for walkin' in on somebody at the wrong time. So you can see I was mighty nervous. I backed my cleaning stuff all the way down the hall and bumped the vacuum cleaner down the stairs to the ground floor, stayin' as far away from the elevator as I could so I wouldn't have to see them people again. What was I gonna say to 'em? What would they say to me? Would Mr. Shields just try to tough it out and wave and greet me in the friendly way he always did, or would he just fire me on the spot? Or was I even going to give him the chance?

Well, I didn't even go back to the top floor that night. I finished what I had to do on the ground floor and got out of there and went on to the clinic where things were pretty quiet for a change, since the police had been keepin' the 'Pro-lifers' in line. And then I went home early.

Sadie, my wife, was still awake when I got there, which is another unusual thing, so we had a beer together in the living room. I was tired, but I really didn't feel like goin' to sleep, and I didn't feel like talkin' to anybody, either. So when Sadie came in in her bathrobe, I poured her a glass of beer as much to slow down the amount of conversation as anything else, but which didn't seem to do much good, since it still didn't take her more than a minute to swing into her usual song and dance about things that needed to be done around the house. "That shutter at the back still needs to be fixed, Braxton. You gonna be able to do it this weekend?"

"Uh, yeah," I said. "I'll get to it."

"It's been broken a long time," she said.

"I'll get to it, Sadie," I said. "I'll get to it."

And then it won't more'n a minute later she looked at me and said, "Braxton, what's wrong with you?"

And I said, "What? What you talkin' about?"

And she said, "You. You're fidgetin' like a worm in hot ashes. What's wrong?"

Now, like I say, I didn't much want to talk about this stuff, but after I took another swallow of beer, I said, "Yeah. All right. I seen sump'n today I'd just as soon not've seen." And I told her the whole story, and then I said, "Now tell me what I'm gonna do next time I see Mr. Shields? And what's he gonna do when he sees me?"

"Oh Lord, Braxton," Sadie said. "If I were you, I wouldn't even go back down there."

"Yeah," I said.

"You don't want to get involved with this in any way at all."

"That's right," I said. "I sure don't. But he does owe me a week's pay."

"Call that secretary in the treasurer's office, get her to mail it to you."

"And then, tell me what I'm gonna say to Mrs. Shields?" I said.

"Mrs. Shields?"

"Yeah. Next time I see her. Am I gonna quit that job, too?....And at the clinic," I said. "What about the clinic? I got that job through Mr. Shields."

"Oh Lord, Braxton!"

"Mrs. Shields is sure to know I'm not workin' at the Corporation anymore. And she's gonna ask me about it."

"Things surely do get complicated, don't they?" Sadie said. And then, all of a sudden, she started to giggle.

"What you laughin' at?"

"It's sort of funny," she said. And then she started to laugh out loud. "Archibald Shields with his britches down!"

"Well I'm glad you find it so amusing," I said.

But by this time she was laughing so hard I thought I was gonna have to carry her to the emergency room. She just slapped her hands and hollered, "Archibald Shields with his britches down! Braxton, do you realize...do you realize this makes you one of the most powerful men in Richmond?"

"What you talkin' about?"

"You've got the goods on Archibald Shields. You know what the newspaper said about him maybe runnin' for the legislature next year. If that news article is right, he'd probably give you anything you want just to go away and keep your mouth shut."

"I don't want to hurt them people, Sadie."

"Yeah. I know it and you know it. But he doesn't know it," Sadie said. And then she started laughing again. "Braxton, I don't think you got anything at all to be afraid of from Archibald Shields."

2

Well, maybe so, maybe no. Sadie might have been right about having nothin' to fear from Archibald Shields, but I know that people will do almost anything to cover their asses these days. And besides that, the situation was a lot more complicated than I've let on so far, so maybe I'd better stop and give you some of the background.

You see, the only reason I was workin' at the Corporation in the first place was because Mrs. Shields had recommended me. I'd been cleaning her house, still do. And I had got that job with her because I'd been recommended by her best friend—which is the way I've got most of my jobs. Mrs. Shields later told me that her friend, Mrs. Archer, told her I was the best house cleaner she'd ever had and that I was "absolutely honest and trustworthy in every way"—which made me feel very good because my daddy and my granddaddy both had always taught me that the best thing any black man had goin' for him was an impeccable reputation. That was my granddaddy's word, *impeccable*. (He taught us a lot of big words—along with takin' off our hats in the house and sayin' 'yes sir' and 'yes ma'm' to our elders.) Anyway, although my own reputation may not have always been as impeccable as I might like (a thing I'll get to later on), it's still a pretty good reputation. But that's just part of it.

You see, after I'd been workin' at the Shields house for a few months, Mrs. Shields stopped me in the kitchen one day after I'd finished polishing the linoleum, and she said, "Braxton, let me ask you something."

"Yes ma'm," I said. "What's that?"

"I hope you don't mind. It's kind of personal," she said.

Now of course, I realized right off that this was not going to be the kind of kitchen conversation we usually had, but I didn't expect anything out of the ordinary, so I leaned back on the counter and said, "Well, I don't have much to hide. What is it?"

And she said, "It's your name."

"My name?"

"Yes," she said, "your name—Braxton Bragg."

"What about my name?"

"Well...this is hard, Braxton," she said. "You have to excuse me. I don't know how to ask it exactly. But you're the first colored man—oh, Braxton, what's right?"

"Ma'm?"

"Colored people? Black people? African American people? When I was growin' up, we called folks either colored people or Negroes, but people have gotten so persnickety I don't know what's right anymore."

Of course, I had to laugh at this, and I said, "Well, I suppose if 'Colored People' is good enough for the NAACP, it's good enough for me."

And she said, "Oh, thank you."

But before she got too comfortable, I said, "Of course, my Uncle Tommy used to tell his boys when they were actin' up, he'd tell 'em, 'A nigger by any other name is still a nigger if he acts like one.'"

"Oh, Braxton, that's terrible!" she said, "terrible."

And I really had to laugh at this. "It didn't seem to hurt 'em," I told her, "since one of 'em turned out to be a lawyer and the other one's dean of that two-year college downtown. So what was it you wanted to know about my name?"

It took her a minute to calm down, but then she said, "You see, what I started out to tell you was that you're the first colored man I know of to be named after a Confederate general."

"Yes ma'm."

"And I wondered where your name came from because before I married Mr. Shields, my name was Bragg, also."

"Oh, I see," I said. Of course, at the moment I didn't really see much. But things were startin' to click through my mind faster than the figures in the cash register down at Ukrop's grocery store as I tried to remember all the stories I'd heard from my daddy and granddaddy. "Well," I said finally, "according to my mother and daddy, I was named Braxton Bragg because General Bragg was my great granddaddy."

And I thought Mrs. Shields was gonna faint right

there. "What?" she said. "General Bragg was...."

"...Was my great granddaddy," I said. "Yes Ma'm."

"Braxton, I can't believe it!"

"Well," I said, "the way I understand it is that General Bragg had several children. One of 'em was named William."

"William?"

"Yes Ma'm."

"I never heard of a William."

"He was the youngest," I said. "And he didn't get along with the rest of the family, so he ran off to a farm down in New Kent County. And that's when he crossed over and married my grandmother. Which explains my lighter complexion," I said.

"Oh My Lord!" Mrs. Shields said. "Oh My Lord!"

She sat down at the kitchen table and got up and sat down again. And then she said, "Braxton, you sit right here and wait a minute. I've got to look up somethin'." And she walked to the front of the house and came back a few minutes later with a book which she opened across the table. And there it was, the whole family tree. "Here," she said. "Here's General Bragg and here are his children. I'm descended from Robert. You can see my name, Lucy, farther down on the page. And here..." She pointed with her finger across the page. "Here is William."

"Yes Ma'm. The people down in New Kent used to call him Billy—Billy Bragg."

"But they don't have anything else in the book about

him," she said. "...no marriage, no children, no date of death...nothing."

"I wonder why that is," I said. And I started to laugh. I thought she might laugh, too, but she was busy lookin' down at the book like she didn't hear me.

And then a minute later she looked up and said, "Braxton, are you sure this is right?"

"Well," I said, "I'm sure my granddaddy was a white man named William Bragg who everybody said was the son of General Bragg."

"But Braxton, if what you're saying is the truth, that makes us third or fourth cousins."

"That's about right," I said. And then I went all out. "You're my cousin Lucy."

And that's when she was able to laugh about it. "Oh my, oh my, oh my! Cousin Lucy and Cousin Braxton. Oh, My Lord!" And she laughed harder. "It surely gives me a new way of looking at things," she said. "A whole new way."

"Yes Ma'm," I said. And then I said, "What do you want to do about it?"

"Do about it? What on earth can be done about it?"

"Do you want me to keep on workin' for you?"

"Well yes, Braxton. Why not? We may as well keep it in the family." And she was laughin' again about the whole thing.

Now, I don't actually know whether or not she ever told Mr. Shields that I was her black cousin. And I haven't told anybody either, except Sadie. Here around Richmond, everybody knows somethin' that we don't talk about. We know it and we all know that we know it, but we just don't mention it. Kind of a social contract, you understand, and everybody seems pretty happy with it. Lucy Shields was good to me and I kept on workin' for her. Sometimes, if we were alone, I'd call her 'Cousin Lucy,' and she'd call me 'Cousin Braxton,' but if anybody else was there, I'd always refer to her as 'Mrs. Shields.' It's the kind of thing you grow to understand around here. Smooths the way, you see. But it wasn't very long afterwards that she recommended me to her husband as somebody to take care of Corporation Headquarters, and I got that job. So you can understand that when I walked in on Mr. Shields and Miss Blowzer, I had a considerable conflict inside. It was the job and the good pay, yes, but it was more than the job and the good pay. It's hard to explain. I mean, I had the key to their house. I took care of everything they had. I sometimes even made up the bed where Mr. Shields slept with Mrs. Shields, and now Archibald Shields was two timin' Lucy who had been good to me. Of course, I know that there are precious few people in this world who haven't done that sort of thing at some time or other, including me, but I didn't want to know it about Archibald Shields.

Anyway, the next day after the big 'interruption' was a Friday, the day I usually picked up my check from the treasurer's office, and I was nervous as a cat. I sure didn't want to see anybody, and I thought maybe I could park my truck in the alley just long enough to pick up my check and leave. So you can imagine my surprise when I looked at my check and found that it was fifty dollars more than usual and that there was a note in the envelope from Mr. Shields sayin', "Braxton, please come by my office before you leave this afternoon."

Just what I didn't want. I went back to the truck to turn on my emergency blinkers, and for a minute I just sat there tryin' to decide what to do, and then I remembered the text the preacher had used on the previous Sunday morning, saying, "Naked came I into the world and naked will I go out of it"—or somethin' pretty close to it. "So, what have I got to lose?" I said to myself. I locked the truck and went back into the building and up the stairs to the second floor, prayin' all the time that I wouldn't run smack into Miss Blowzer when I got there, and you can guess my relief when I just found Mrs. Welford by herself in the outer office.

"Oh Braxton, yes," Mrs. Welford said. "Mr. Shields wants to see you." And she went to his door to tell him I was outside.

Well, it wasn't more than a couple of seconds before he came out to meet me, all cordial and smiling, and shook my hand and said, "Braxton, I'm glad to see you. Come in."

He led me into his office and motioned for me to sit in one of the big soft chairs in front of his desk—right in front of the spot where he and Miss Blowzer had been gettin' it on the day before—and he said, "Since most of us go home before you come to work, we hardly ever get to see you. How have you been?"

"I've been all right," I said.

"Anything you need to help you do your job better?"

"Can't think of anything right off," I said. "Except maybe it might be good if I could hire another person to help me, especially since your staff has increased so much in the past year."

"Well, that might be a possibility," he said. "Do you know a person?"

"I'll have to look," I said. "It's tricky business finding someone who's trustworthy."

"Yes, it certainly is," he said. "And that was my main reason for asking you to drop by today—to tell you how much we appreciate you and your work. Because, as I'm sure you know, this day and time, it's so hard to find someone who does good work and is trustworthy. And I wanted you to know you had not been overlooked."

"Er...that is good to know," I said.

"And I suppose you noticed the extra fifty dollars in your paycheck this time."

"I did, yes sir."

"Well that will stay there, and at the end of the quarter, I think we can add another fifty dollars, as a token of our appreciation."

"That's very good," I said. "And I appreciate it. I really do."

"Because, as you know," he said, "man to man, there is nothing more valuable than a co-worker who does good work and is trustworthy." And then he looked across at me and smiled the biggest ol' shit-eatin' grin I ever saw in my life. And I smiled back at him. But I knew it was time for me to get up and go on to my next job.

3

Now, I know that I am not the first nigger in this town to be bought and paid for. But the whole thing made me feel kind of weird. Money's good. And for a guy like me who's spent a lot of his life without it, I sure ain't gonna turn it down. But it's one thing to be paid for your work and another thing to be paid for your silence, for your fidelity. That's another word my granddaddy taught me—*fidelity*, along with *impeccable* reputation. "Have fidelity, Boy," he used to say, "be faithful to something. Be faithful to yourself mostly, 'cause if you're not faithful to yourself, you can bet nobody else is gonna be." Of course, there was no way in hell that I as a boy could know what he meant by all that, and I'm not sure I've got more than a slim notion about it now.

But while I'm talking about fidelity and reputation, let me just tell you something and get it off my chest before somebody comes up and calls me a phony. I've got a police record. It happened over thirty years ago, and not many people remember it anymore, but it's there if somebody wanted to dig for it. So let me tell you. It happened when I was a senior in high school, in the wintertime right after I turned eighteen. I was gettin' ready to go home after school one day, and when I went into the cloakroom to get my coat off the rack, my coat was gone. Now, like I told you before,

we were a country family, a farming family, and we didn't have a lot of money, but my mama and daddy always managed to see that the kids had decent clothes to wear, and that overcoat was brand new. I liked that overcoat. I expected to wear that coat lookin' for jobs after I graduated or maybe even wear it to college if I was able to get in like my older brother Billy did. So losing that coat really tore me up. I reported it as stolen, of course, but I wanted to do more than that. My daddy had never hesitated to use the flat of his hand against me to keep me in line, and I wanted to keep other people in line, too. So when about three days after the coat disappeared, the fool that stole it wore it to school, I think you can understand my reaction when I saw him. His name was Sammy and I yelled down the hall at him, "Sammy, I want to talk to you." I remember the whole thing like it was yesterday. "That's my coat you're wearin'," I told him.
"No it ain't," he said. "It's my coat."

"Don't bullshit me," I said. "I know my coat when I see it, and I want it back." And right about then he took off running, which he should have known better than to do since I had been the fastest man on the track team that year. I chased him down the hall and into a classroom where I cornered him and he took a swing at me, and that's when I let fly. I ducked his swing and came up with a hard right to his jaw and knocked him back over a desk, and then he rolled to the side and came back at me. We fought across that classroom and on out into the hall where I finally backed him up against the water cooler and beat the living hell out of him.

Oh it was a scene! I was still workin' on him when the security guards came in and grabbed me from behind. "He stole my overcoat," I told them.

And they said, "You can tell that to the judge." And they clamped handcuffs on me, charged me with "aggravated assault," and carried me off to the jailhouse. I found out later that I broke the guy's jaw and knocked out some teeth and had even gotten blood all over my overcoat in the process. But since I was over eighteen, the judge saw my assault as rather serious and fined me a hundred dollars, which my daddy had to pay, and gave me a nice lecture about not trying to take the law into my own hands.

So there it is, I have a police record. Changed my way of lookin' at the world, I can tell you, because a lot of doors slammed shut to me that day, or I thought they did. I learned that not every person convicted of a crime is a crook and not every crook is convicted of a crime—or convicted of anything else, for that matter, since most of the crooks in this world seem to get off. But people like labels. And a young guy with a record learns pretty quick that when he fills out a job application and comes to the question: "Have you ever been convicted of a crime?" that he may as well throw the application in the trash and keep on walkin'.

My granddaddy died shortly after that, and he was not around to explain to me exactly how I was supposed to maintain my fidelity and my impeccable reputation after a conviction. That was something I had to try and learn by myself over the years. And one of the things I started learning how to do was to control my temper.

Being arrested had really scared me. I had felt those handcuffs on my wrists and seen the jailhouse close up, and I didn't want any more of it. My temper didn't go away, but I pushed it down. I became 'Mr. Peacemaker'," doin' everything I could to avoid trouble before it started—even when I finally went to work with some pretty rough dudes, first in the tobacco fields and then on some construction jobs.

You see, although I didn't really understand it at the time, I was 'different' from a lot of the guys I worked with. To start with, I was lighter than most of the black guys, but of course, not quite light enough to suit the white guys. And then, on top of that, since my granddaddy was a white man and both my parents had finished high school, I grew up speaking a kind of English that was different from almost everybody around me, especially different from the guys who came from Southside Virginia and spoke a dialect they called Kohee that was so thick even I couldn't understand it at first. They laughed at me and called me 'Whitey' for tryin' to act like the white man, they said. But even though I wanted to knock the shit out of whoever said this, I didn't. I just learned to talk like they did, and before long, I could out-nigger the best of 'em. I told 'em jokes and I laughed with them and began to get along with 'em pretty good.

But it didn't take me long to get tired of that stuff, tired of them and tired of the tobacco worms and the smashed fingers I got workin' construction. So when my Aunt Mary needed somebody to help her in a housekeeping job she had, I was ready to go. She took me to the home of Dr. Robert Moncure who had a big summer house right on the bank of the Chicahominy River, and that's where my house cleaning career began—which now, near'bout forty years later, I call the Bragg Janitorial Service.

But I'm getting away from my story of that week when all hell started breaking loose in Richmond. That Friday afternoon right after I had my meeting with Mr. Shields, I went to the Sharon Clinic for Women. Friday was the day they stayed open till nine o'clock, and Dr. Redman, one of the guys that ran the place, had asked me to come in early because all of a sudden like, the anti-abortion people had started picketing the place again. "We can get police protection during business hours," Dr. Redman told me, "but I don't think it would be safe for you to be here after that—at least not tonight."

So I got down there between four and five o'clock, and it was wild, I tell you. The pickets were walkin' around the place, some carrying signs in their hands, some with signs on sandwich boards hanging around their necks, signs saying things like, "Abortion is Murder," and "It's not a choice, it's a baby," and "Jesus said, 'Suffer the little children to come unto me,'" and "You are a generation of vipers!" and on and on. The people with the viper signs were especially hot in trying to get close to any woman who went into the place, shouting at her, calling her such things as "Scarlet Woman!" "Jezebel," "Baby killer," "Murderer!"

You name it. And of course, the police had their hands full trying to keep a safe distance between the pickets and the clients of the place. They stopped me, of course, when I tried to drive into the parking lot, askin' all sorts of questions, Who was I? Why was I there? and being really nasty about it in the process, not wanting to believe I worked there till one of the nurses stuck her head out and identified me. It makes anybody nervous to be grilled by a bunch of pushy cops, but I found out that it was nothin' compared to the trouble I was getting myself into by just driving onto the grounds that day.

In any case, I had my hands full from the moment I walked into the place, and none of the work was what I had ever thought of as 'janitorial.' "Braxton, are we ever glad to see you!" the head nurse said as I came in the door. Her name was Frances, and she was a pistol. "We've got only one doctor and he's backed up till after nine o'clock; the nurses have got their hands full, and we've got a big problem in the ladies' room," she told me all in one long breath.

"What's the matter in the ladies' room?" I said, thinkin' maybe a commode was stopped up or something.

But she said, "It's a woman."

"A woman?"

"Yeah, the mother of one of the patients. She's barricaded herself in there and won't do anything but curse and shout when we ask her to come out."

"Um hum," I said. And I had to give it some thought because the idea of bustin' into the ladies' room to drag out a crazy woman was not appealing to me at all. "You've got plenty of policemen outside," I said. "Maybe...."

But Frances didn't even let me finish. "I thought of that," she said. "But a policeman has got to make a report, and if the newspaper picks it up, we're liable to be in bigger trouble than we are now. Let's see if we can handle it ourselves." And she led me around the corner to the ladies' room and knocked on the locked door. "Mrs. Smith...?" she said.

And the screamin' that came back from inside the ladies' room would take the paint off the wall. "God damn it! I told you to go away and leave me alone!" Mrs. Smith said.

"We have to get into the restroom, Mrs. Smith."

"Leave me alone!"

"Other people have to use it."

But Mrs. Smith came back louder than ever, calling Frances every kind of bitch that had ever crawled the earth.

"If you don't come out, we're going to break the door down," Frances said, and with that 'we' she was, of course, volunteering my services.

"Sounds like she's drunk," I said.

"God knows," Frances said, "but let's get her out. Her daughter is ready to go home and we need her bed space." And she motioned me toward the door.

It was a hollow plywood door and I knew it wouldn't be any great problem to break it, but I held back. "I'd appreciate it if we had one other person to witness this," I said.

"Why? Don't you trust me?" Frances said.

"I've just always found there's safety in numbers," I said. And I was smiling when I said it.

"OK," she said. "OK." She called another nurse, but I could tell she was put out with me because I didn't just heave to and do what she told me. The second nurse was a pretty little black girl named Alice. "Braxton wants you to see how strong he is when he breaks this God damned door down," Frances said. Alice sort of snickered, and I didn't say anything, and then Frances said, "OK, Braxton, let's see what you can do."

It didn't take but two big heaves from my shoulder and one hard kick to break the lock loose from the wall, but all the while Mrs. Smith was on the inside callin' me every kind of son of a bitch you could think of, and then when the door finally did give way, she came out like an angry cat clawing at my face. Course, I had to defend myself, and in less than a second I was rollin' on the floor tryin' to control this angry white woman who I realized by then was drunk out her mind. I was tryin' to control her body and her legs and the nurses were trying to control her hands until finally I got what you might call a half nelson on her and said, "Would somebody please call the police!" And Alice ran to the door and waved a cop into the building.

It's amazing how the sight of a blue uniform can calm people down. Mrs. Smith stopped struggling the minute she saw the cop, but of course she told him that I was a damned pervert who broke the door open and tried to get at her as soon as she went into the ladies' room. But the nurses straightened this out and the policeman had some sense, thank God. He looked in the ladies' room and picked up an empty whiskey bottle. "Is this yours?" he said.

And Mrs. Smith said, "No, Officer. I don't drink."

The whole place smelled like a brewery, of course, and the policeman said, "No, of course not. But if you don't calm down and leave this building, I'm going to arrest you for being drunk and disorderly, anyway."

"I can't leave," she said. And she began to cry. "I have to get my daughter and she's in there having surgery and it's just awful! I came here with my daughter so I could drive her home safely."

The policeman was a young guy, but when he looked up at the rest of us, he had the saddest and most hopeless look I've ever seen on a man's face.

"She's ready," Frances said. "Come on, Braxton, let's go get her daughter."

"Me? Why me?" I said.

"Because we're over crowded and we had to put her upstairs."

"Oh," I said, and I followed Frances up the steps.

The girl was lying there on a gurney all pale and frightened when we got there. "Are you ready to go home?" Frances said.

"I guess so," the girl told her.

And then, after the girl was standing, Frances said, "I don't like your color. Maybe we'd better carry you down."

And she turned to me again and said, "Braxton, can you carry her?"

The girl wasn't big, weighed maybe a hundred pounds. "Sure," I said, "but you'd better go in front of me just in case."

So I scooped up this girl. She was even lighter than I thought, and we started down the stairs with Frances backing down in front of me, and everything was going OK until nearly at the bottom when somethin' inside the girl gave way and I could feel a warm liquid suddenly soaking through the front of my pants. "Oh holy shit!" Frances said. She called Alice, and a minute later the two of them had rolled up another gurney for me to put the girl on and then they pushed her into the main operating room with the doctor and closed the door.

Of course, when I looked down, I saw that my pants were just soaked with the girl's blood. "Jesus!" I said. I don't usually talk that way but I did on that day, "Oh Jesus!" I looked at the policeman who was still there with the girl's mother. "Can you stick around?" I asked him, "at least until this one's over?"

"Sure," he said. "I'd hate to think this woman was going to do any driving today."

"Yeah," I said. "OK. I'll be here to help, but while we wait, I'm going to start taking some of this trash out."

"Right," the policeman said.

It took them another hour to get the girl stabilized. She was a bleeder, Frances told me later, but they got her under control, and then the policeman and I escorted the girl and her mother out through the picket line that began to come to life the minute they saw her. Sounded like a pack of hounds at feeding time, yelling, "Baby killer!" and "Murderer!" and raising an awful din there on the corner.

The policeman was a nice young guy named Collins, and he drove the two of them home in his squad car while I followed in the woman's car till we got 'em back to their apartment down on Grace Street. Then I came back to the clinic with Officer Collins, and even though I had got there early that day, it took me till near'bout midnight to clean up the place and carry out the rest of the trash.

4

The thing that started getting to me that night, though, was the nature of the trash. You know, in the years I'd been workin' at the clinic, I had just carried away whatever they told me to. I carried out those red plastic bags marked 'Biohazard' the same way I carried out waste paper from the trash baskets down at the corporation. But that night, with that girl's blood growing stiff as it dried on the front of my pants, I began to see something else. It's one thing to call something a bio-hazard but quite another thing to call it human remains. And that night, I realized as never before that the bags I was carrying out to my truck were filled with human remains—embryos, fetuses, some a lot more advanced than most people wanted to admit. And I was hauling them off to the dump. Man! That began to give me the willies. And after the way the anti-abortion picketers had been acting that day, I started disguising every one of them red bags inside another black plastic bag so they wouldn't be so easy to spot.

This, I realized later, was a wise thing to do, but like a lot of our wise decisions, it came too late. Because that day, just by driving into the parking lot at the clinic, I played right into the hands of the pro-lifers. They got my license number. And in less than twelve hours, they had traced it and found out who I was and where I lived, and then they called me at home about seven o'clock the next morning. I mean, these people never sleep. Sadie was in the shower when the phone rang, and I answered, still half asleep from workin' late the night before, and this man's voice said, "Brother, I want you to know that we're praying for you to see the light and leave that sinful clinic."

"Who in the hell are you?" I said. But he didn't even hesitate.

"I speak with the voice of one who gives you a chance for salvation, Brother, a chance to help stamp out the sinful murder of little children."

"How did you get my number?" I said.

But he went right on, "I'm going to give you a number to call so you can help us on the winning side, Braxton, because sooner or later we are going to win this war, and the people who're with us will be rewarded and those who are against us will suffer the tortures of the damned." And then he reeled off this long distance telephone number. "We're praying for you to call us," he said and hung up.

Well now, I thought, what the hell was I going to do with that? And what did he mean by the "tortures of the damned?" Was that a threat or just his way of talking? And then, just about the time Sadie came out of the shower and started getting dressed for work, the telephone rang again, and this time it was a woman's voice. "Braxton," she said, "we want you to know that we're counting on you to do the right thing."

"Who are you?" I said.

But she went right on, "I know that you're a good man, and I don't want to see you get hurt. But we need your help. So call us at this number and give us some information. That's all we want, just some information." Then she gave me another number.

"Who was that?" Sadie said when I hung up.

"I don't know," I told her, "but I think I've just been threatened."

"Threatened?!"

"Yeah. By people who don't want me to work down at the clinic."

"Oh, My Lord, Braxton! It's gettin' dangerous to live with you."

"Yeah," I said. "Well, you ought to try being me for a day."

But things were quiet for the rest of the morning. Sadie went on to work, and I went on to my house cleaning day jobs. But the newspaper was full of stories and pictures of the clinic with all the picketers marching around, and there in one of the pictures was a photo of my truck with the license plate shining in clear view. And that's when I realized how they learned who I was.

Well, that was the afternoon I usually went to the Shields's house, not for a full cleaning job that day but just to take out the trash and neaten up for the weekend. I went on over there in the early afternoon, driving through Windsor Farms and on to their house that sits back near the river, and no sooner did I park the truck in the yard than their seventeen-year-old daughter Betsy came running out to meet me.

Now let me tell you about Betsy. She is their 'late life' child, born after her older brother and sister had grown up and moved away. And she is a ticking time bomb lookin' for a place to explode. Of course, Mr. and Mrs. Shields think that Betsy is God's greatest gift to humanity since Jesus Christ, and they'll do most anything she wants. She goes to one of those fancy private schools in the West End, and all through that year she had been telling me how she was going to have this big "coming out" party the following season. I don't know exactly what she was coming out from under because she already left very little hidden from view. I mean, she had this knockout figure that she seemed very proud of, and she liked to wear these skimpy little mini-skirts or short shorts, I guess you'd call 'em, along with a tee shirt and no underwear. Or she wore a blouse that buttoned down the front and usually left half the buttons unhooked. You get the picture, and a pretty complete picture it was.

Anyway, on this day, she came running out to meet me, wearing this half buttoned blouse, and she threw her arms around my neck and hugged me, the way she'd lately taken to doing, and rubbed herself all over me, sayin' something about her party dress. "Braxton, why are you so late? The dressmaker just brought my new ball gown to try on, and I would have shown it to you but she's already gone."

"Well, I know you must have looked mighty pretty,"

I said. And I tried to pull away from her, but it looked like the more I pulled away, the tighter she held on.

Let me tell you, this kind of thing makes me mighty nervous. I didn't want nothin' to do with this girl, you understand. But she was a sexy girl and I am a man, and when a sexy girl starts rubbing herself up against me, well...it gives me problems. Of course, my natural instinct was to put my arm around her waist and walk on into the house with her and see what would have happened next, but I didn't do it. I just crammed my hands in my pockets so I wouldn't be touching her at all.

Not that I had anything against white girls, you understand. I remember thirty or thirty-five years ago when I was a young guy and workin' at night as an orderly in a nursing home, there were two white nurses who thought I was the hottest thing since vegetable soup. One was named Patty and the other was Barbara—or Barb, as she called herself. Well, late at night, I'd ride upstairs in the elevator with Barb, and just before we'd get to the top floor, she'd reach up and stop the elevator, and a minute later she'd be out of her clothes and we'd be goin' at it. I mean, she really liked this quickie stuff. Bammo! Whammo! And then, in less time than it takes to tell about it, she'd be back in her nurse's uniform, all crisp and fresh lookin' like nothin' had happened at all when she stepped out on the third floor two minutes later. Then I'd come back downstairs and there'd be Patty, who'd pull me into an empty room and close the door and it'd be the same thing all over again, except layin' down. I had quite a career there as the 'elevator man' until the two of 'em found out what was goin' on and made my life such hell, I had to quit my job. But this thing with Betsy was different and dangerous. Not only was she a young girl who didn't know what the hell she was doin', but she was the boss's daughter. And I knew that there have not been many courts in the American South that have ever convicted a white man for shooting a black man who, he thought, was molesting his under age daughter. Certainly not if the white man was rich. And I didn't want to be the next victim of that trap.

"You better let me go now so I can get my stuff out the truck," I said, and I started peeling Betsy's arms away from my neck.

"Braxton, I don't think you like me," Betsy said.

And I said, "Honey, I like you fine, but your mama is expecting me to go to work right away, and I don't want to disappoint her." And I pulled loose while she kept on chattering about her party dress.

As it turned out, her mama really was glad to see me because just before I walked in, she had turned over a bottle of milk on the kitchen floor and that was my first job of the day—cleanin' up spilt milk.

Betsy had followed me in, of course, bouncy and sassy as you please while I was lookin' for the mop, and she said, "Mama, Braxton doesn't like me."

But Lucy Shields had more sense than to pay attention to this foolishness. "Now you just run on and leave Braxton alone," she said. "He's got enough to worry about without you bothering him." And then she turned to me and said, "And Braxton, when you get through, I want to talk to you about something else before you go."

Of course, under the circumstances, that gave me somewhat of a chill right there, but as it turned out, what she wanted to do was offer me another job. I finished taking out the trash and generally straightening up the house, and then I found her in the living room. "Sit down," she said. "Listen. The Museum is getting ready to have a great big celebration, and it's a chance for you to make some good money, if you're interested."

"Tell me more," I said.

And then she told me how the Museum of Fine Arts was planning to put on this big fund raising banquet and dance to celebrate the opening of their exhibit of Russian art and jewelry—"Faberge design," I think she called it. "It'll be the biggest thing the Museum has ever done, and we'll need a lot of people to help us beforehand and to clean up afterward. Are you interested?"

"Well, I do have my other jobs," I said.

"I'll see that you get paid a thousand dollars for the two or three days it'll take."

"Oh well," I said, "I expect I can move a few things around to fit the schedule."

"Good," she said. "Good. I'll tell you more about it later. Do you know how to tend bar?"

"Yes," I said. "I learned when I worked for Doctor Moncure a long time ago."

"All right. We may want you to tend bar. Do you have a tuxedo?"

"No."

"Well don't worry about it. If you need a tuxedo, we'll get you one."

"I'll try anything once," I said. And then I went on to my next job thinkin' that it is good to have friends in high places, after all.

The rest of that day was pretty calm compared to the day before. When I got to the clinic right at closing time there were only a couple of tired and seedy lookin' picketers walkin' around with their signs on the street outside and there wasn't much of a crowd inside either. The only thing new that day was that Alice, the pretty little nurse, met me at the door and took my arm as I walked in with my stuff. "Braxton," she said, "I want to tell you how much I admire what you did yesterday."

"Just part of the job," I said.

"Maybe," she said. "But you did some hard things. I don't think we could have handled it without you."

"Well, I appreciate you sayin' that," I told her.

"I just wanted you to know that I knew," she said. And she looked up at me and blinked her eyes in a way that near'bout gave me a heart attack right there just as Frances walked into the room.

"Er...well, I guess I'd better get on to work," I said. And then I thought maybe I ought to tell 'em about the telephone calls I got.

"Oh my God, Braxton," Frances said when I told

'em, "I never thought they'd do that to you."

"Well they did."

"That's why we never use anything but our first names," Alice said. "And we never drive our own cars to work. Did you tell 'em anything?"

"No," I said, "I didn't give 'em nothin'."

"Well, please don't," Frances said. "We'd never have another minute's peace— around here or at home either—ever again."

Of course, as I went to work, I did have to wonder why nobody had ever bothered to warn me about the dangers of driving my truck into the lot in broad daylight, but I guess people can't think of everything.

In any case, I finished up a couple of hours later without any more trouble around the clinic, but as I drove out of the lot that night, I noticed that a car parked on the street started up and came along behind me just as I turned on to North Boulevard. I didn't think anything about it at the time. I was thinking more about the way Alice was lookin' at me and about how good a doughnut and coffee would taste if I stopped at the donut shop before I went on out to clean the karate studio on West Broad Street. But then I noticed that everywhere I turned, that same car was staying behind me. It had a funny kind of parking lights on its bumper that made it easy to spot in the dark. I even circled around a block to see if it would stay with me. And it did. And I thought, oh, shit! what is this gonna be? I would have speeded up and tried to lose him, but the traffic was too heavy. And then I came to the donut shop where I wanted to stop.

Of course, by this time, remembering those phone calls I got earlier in the day, my pulse was racin' somethin' fierce. But it looked like there was only one person in the other car and I figured I could handle whatever it was. So I pulled into the alley behind the donut shop and drove on through the parking lot with that car following me until I pulled into a narrow space between a row of cars and stopped. Then just as that other car pulled into the trap I'd set for him, I jumped out of my truck and ran back to jerk his door open. "Listen, you son of a bitch," I said, "why are you following me?"

It was then that I realized I was lookin' straight into the eyes of a Roman Catholic priest. He was sittin' there all pasty and white with his reversed collar around his throat, and I swear he was trembling when he spoke. "I want to talk to you," he said. "The church needs your help with that abortion clinic."

And that's when I lit into him again. "Well you listen to me, mutha-fucker. You have just done all the talkin' you're gonna do. I want you to put this car in gear and back your white ass out of here and leave me alone. And if I ever lay eyes on you again, I will beat the livin' shit out of you. Do you understand me?!"

I slammed the door, and he crammed that car into reverse and floor boarded it on the way out of that parkin' lot—even dented somebody's fender as he got to the street. I hated to talk to a priest that way, but the son of a bitch made me mad.

When I told Sadie about it after I got home that night, she just looked at me and said, "Braxton, are you crazy!? Jerkin' somebody's door open in the middle of the night!? Suppose the man had a gun." And then she said, "Have you heard the afternoon news?"

"No," I said. "I been workin'. I ain't heard nothin'."

"Well," she said, "for your information, somebody walked into an abortion clinic in Baltimore this afternoon and shot a doctor and two nurses. These people are serious, Braxton."

5

Of course, by the next morning, the radio and the TV and the newspaper were all filled with the story of the Baltimore massacre. Seems it was done by a bunch of folks who claimed to be doing God's work by saving the unborn children of the world. Course, it appeared to me that they'd do God's work a lot better if they tried to save a few of the children that were already born, but that ain't the way they saw it. The cops had arrested one of the two gunmen, and he had confessed without so much as a blink of his eye or a shiver of guilt. "I killed these people because they're evildoers," he said. "If the law won't stop them, we have to stop them." And then, he was quoted as saying, "Let this be a warning to everybody who works in an abortion clinic: we are coming to get you, wherever you are." And he went into all this crazy religious stuff about how "the sword of Gideon was going to strike on the side of the Lord."

Well, whether these people were really crazy or not, I couldn't tell, but I could sure tell that they were dangerous. One of the gunmen was still at large, and it was clear to me that if they could kill doctors and nurses with such ease, they wouldn't hesitate an instant over a janitor. Dr. Redman called a meeting the next day for everybody who worked at the clinic in order to draw up some emergency plans. Alice called me at home about it, and I went on down there. It was about the end of August or early September, and behind the clinic there was a big crepe myrtle tree looking as peaceful as you please, like there was no problem or anything disturbing goin' on anywhere in the world. Tree just full of red flowers and a lot of little bees buzzin' around. I hadn't even noticed it before, since I worked mostly at night, and I was just standin' there lookin' at how pretty it was when Alice came out the door and called to me. "I'm glad you could make it," she said.

And I said, "Yeah. Well. This kind of stuff makes you think." And I walked on into the clinic with her and told her about the priest who was followin' me around town. "I'm not sure how much more of this I can take," I told her.

"You're not going to desert us, are you?" she said.

"Well, I hate to think of it that way," I said, "but this place is turnin' into a combat zone."

"Braxton...."

She started, but I interrupted her. "Looks like we ought to get hazardous duty pay to work around here."

"Listen," she said. And she really got excited as we walked into the waiting room. "We can't do without you. We're providing a service that people really need. And it's not all abortions. It's fertility counseling and birth control information and education for disease prevention. We can't close down and ignore these people, Braxton."

Now, of course, I sympathized with what she was sayin'. I could remember when Dr. Harry Snow did abortions in a house over on Dove Street in the days before abortions were legal. Some of my family had moved into the North Side of Richmond by that time, and they knew lots of women who went to see Dr. Snow and more than one who'd died after being treated. So I knew something about how bad the abortion situation had been in the old days, and I wanted to help these people, if I could. But good will goes only just so far.

"Who would we get to replace you that we could trust?" Alice said. And she looked up and smiled at me the way she had the day before. "Please don't quit us," she said. "Please."

And like the fool I sometimes am when a pretty woman starts smiling at me, I said, "Naw, I guess I won't...at least not right away." And l smiled back at her the way she had been smiling at me, and of course, I had to tease her a little bit. "But I do hope for a little bonus one day," I said. "You know, a little bonus to go along with my pay check."

"Braxton, you are a mess," she said, "a real mess." And she laughed. Had a real pretty laugh.

But before I could say anything else, Dr. Redman came in with the police chief and a couple of detectives to talk about security measures we could take.

Well, let me tell you about security. They did take steps to strengthen the doors and add metal bars to the windows and set up methods to identify everybody who came on the property. And all this was good, especially during the daytime. But I was still the guy who came to work after hours on most days. I couldn't clean the place while people were still messin' it up, so it was usually well after dark before I got there, specially in the winter time. I would back my truck up as close as I could get it to the door in order to unload my cleaning stuff and load on the trash that I was haulin' to the dump. But still, comin' and goin', back and forth from my truck to the doorway, I became the easiest means anybody could find for getting into the place.

Now, with the 'pro-lifers' raising so much hell and threatening everybody around the country, it was easy to lose sight of something else that was important. Drugs. I was workin' in a medical clinic, after all, where surgical operations were daily performed and where prescription drugs were dispensed and where all the drugs usually kept in a hospital were stored. And I'm sure a lot of folks came to see that clinic as a potential treasure chest of happiness, if they could just get inside.

I was starting to work one night a few days after my run-in with the Catholic priest, and I was bringin' in my vacuum and my mops and all, and to make things easier, I propped the main door open so I wouldn't have to unlock it every time. I had gone back to the truck to get my floor polisher, and I was standing at the tailgate, reachin' over to get the thing, when all of a sudden this crazy lookin' nigger come bustin' out of the shadows from between the dumpster and the crepe myrtle tree waving a butcher knife. I'm not kiddin' you. Damn knife had a blade on it about ten inches long, and he was wavin' it and comin' toward me and shoutin', "Stay out of my way, mutha fucker! Stay out of my way!" He had this long, stringy hair like those guys from down in the islands, and even in that dim light I could see the crazy look in his eyes. He was between me and the open door of the clinic, and backin' toward it.

"Hold on right where you are!" I yelled at him, "You can't go in there!" I don't know where I got the courage to do anything but run, unless it was remembering the way Alice told me how much they depended on me, because I didn't have nothin' to defend myself with but an eighty-pound floor polisher. But I was determined the bastard wasn't gonna get inside that clinic. And then, of course, I near'bout changed my mind when he stopped and came back toward me with the edge of that butcher knife reflecting the glint of the street light every time he waved it. "You are a dead man, cock sucker! You are dead!" he was yellin'.

And that's when I remembered the tire iron.

It's one of those times when laziness really paid off. 'Cause a couple of days earlier, I'd had a flat tire, and then, after I'd changed it, instead of putting the tire tools back in the slot where they belonged, I'd just dropped 'em in the back of the truck. So when I saw that crazy fucker comin' toward me with the butcher knife, I reached down deep in the truck, groping for anything I could get my hands on but hoping for the tire iron and praying that it hadn't shifted around toward the front, and I tell you, nothin' ever felt so good in my life as that piece of cold steel. I grabbed it up by the flat end just as he got to me, and I brought it down right on his knife hand.

Heard the bones of his wrist crack when I hit him. He yelled and the knife went skittering off in the dark somewhere, but I was just gettin' started. My next shot was up side his head, and he went down on his knees, and then I came back from the other direction—whop! This time he went down flat and just laid there moanin' and groanin', and he must have been a tough son of a bitch 'cause it's a wonder to me I didn't have his brains spattered all over the wall. "All right, mutha fucker," I said. "Now let's see what's what." And I was just about to come down on his head again, but I didn't. Somethin' made me stop. Don't know what exactly. I guess I didn't want him to die on the premises with me there. So I grabbed him by the collar and dragged him out to the street and dropped him in the gutter. He was up on his knees tryin' to crawl away by the time I got back to the door, and I never saw him again.

But that night taught me something. Mainly it was that these days, if you move around by yourself in Richmond after dark, you'd better go strapped with something more than a friendly smile. I mean, that whole thing got to me. And the next day I went down to see my cousin Frank who is a lawyer and works in the same law firm that is operated by the mayor of our city, Cliff Eastman.

I didn't make an appointment. I just found the place down on Marshall Street on the way to my first job, and walked in past the brass plaque on the door that said, "Eastman, Bragg, and Riggins." And of course, the first person I saw was Mayor Eastman comin' out from the back office all covered with smiles, and he recognized me right off—as well he should because we used to go to the same Baptist church before he got fancy and went over to the Episcopal Church. "Braxton," he said, reachin' out to shake my hand and slappin' me on the shoulder while he talked, "haven't seen you in a long time."

And I said, "Yes, Cliff. It has been a long time, ain't it? Course, you'd see me a lot more if you'd come back to your own church once in a while."

"Now, Braxton," he said, "I go back. Go back regularly. But you know how it is," and by now he was tappin' me on the chest with his fist. "You have to spread yourself pretty thin tryin' to keep everybody happy."

"I know that must be hard for you," I said.

And then, he was suddenly all business. "Were you coming to see me?"

"No," I said. "I wanted to see my cousin Frank."

"Oh," he said. And he looked a little disappointed, but he smiled again and introduced me to the secretary and told her to take care of me, and he went on out the door.

Frank was cordial, but he seemed nervous, just kept standing behind his desk like he didn't want me to get too comfortable. "I can't see you for long," he said. "I've got a client coming in ten minutes."

"Well, ten minutes is all I need," I said. And then I looked at him standin' there fidgeting in his thousand-dollar suit and said, "It is all right if I sit down, ain't it?"

"Oh yes, yes of course," Frank said. "Sit down."

So I sat and told him about being assaulted the night before. "I need a gun," I said. "And a concealed carry permit. Tell me how to get 'em."

"Well, the gun's no problem. Just go to the store and buy one. They'll do a quick background check."

"I'd just as soon nobody knew I had it," I said.

"Then you'll have to buy it second hand from somebody. As for the permit, you need to pay $75 dollars and show the court that you've had training from a licensed instructor. Then it'll take about sixty days while they check up on every time you have ever even sneezed in public."

"Unh hunh," I said, thinkin' about that time I was arrested for assault when I was eighteen.

"I don't advise you to carry a gun, Braxton."

"OK," I said. "But then tell me what I'm supposed to do next time somebody comes after me with a butcher knife and I don't happen to have a tire iron in my pocket."

"Well, as I remember, you used to be a track star in high school. I bet you can still run faster than most men."

"Thanks for the advice," I said. And I was about to stand up when the intercom buzzed on his desk and the secretary was tellin' him that his next client had arrived.

"I'm sorry, Braxton," Frank said. "But I do have to see this man."

"Oh, I won't hold you," I told him. "I was just gettin' ready to go." He was sitting forward on the edge of his chair like he was eager to jump up and help me out the door. But for some reason, probably out of pure meanness, I just sat there for another minute. "How's your brother Clarence?" I said, speaking slowly, you know, stretching it out.

"Oh, Clarence is doing fine," Frank said. "I guess you heard he's dean of the college now."

"Yeah. That's what I heard. Gettin' to be a mighty big man," I said. "I tried to talk to him last time I saw him at church, but he was so busy talkin' to some white folks he'd brought over there, I realized he wasn't gonna have time to talk to me. And then, I saw him driving away in a new Mercedes."

"Oh yeah," Frank said. "He's crazy about that Mercedes. Told me he was going to get another one for his daughter."

"He's gonna get two Mercedes!?"

"Yeah," Frank said. "But that's Clarence. He's a very big man now."

I stood then and started out—having had about enough of 'big men' for one morning. But then at the door, I stopped. That whole meeting with Frank had sort of put me on edge. And I looked back at him and said, "You know, Frank, seeing Clarence with his white friends and driving his Mercedes...sometimes I think your brother Clarence don't want to know any other niggers."

"Why Braxton, what a thing to say!"

"Yeah. Well. I bet you know some men like that, too," I said. "Looks like Clarence has got to the place where he don't want to know any other niggers. And in fact, I get the feeling that Clarence don't even want to admit that he's a nigger himself. But he is." And then I walked out.

I guess it was a mean thing to say, but I'm glad I said it. People can make you feel bad if you let 'em. And sometimes you just have to say what's on your mind.

I was still frettin' about Frank in his thousand-dollar suit and Clarence with his two Mercedes as I walked out of the building. But by the time I got to my truck, it was clear to me that if I was going to buy a pistol on my own terms, I had to use something other than conventional means. I didn't know for sure whether that conviction for assault when I was eighteen would keep me from buying a gun commercially or not, but frankly, I just didn't want to take the chance of having some wise-assed store clerk tell me he couldn't sell me a gun because of my record.

Still, I figured all was not lost. "Perseverance overcometh all things," my granddaddy used to say. That was another one of his favorite words, *perseverance*, along with *impeccable* and *fidelity*. Well, I might be a little short on the impeccable reputation part, but perseverance I still had, and the first thing I thought of was my older brother, Billy. Course, since he's a teacher in one of the local high schools, I knew I couldn't see him till the end of the day. So I went on over to clean Mrs. Archer's house. You may remember that Mrs. Archer is the one that introduced me to the Shields family in the first place, and she is married to Beaumont Archer who's the boss of one of the biggest stock market outfits in this city. Investment banker, I guess you'd call him. Anyway, she came to the door with the telephone in her hand,

and she seemed all excited and distressed about something, but she motioned for me to come on into the kitchen while she went right on talking.

Now, I wasn't eavesdropping or trying to horn in on her private conversation or anything. I was just bringing in my cleaning stuff, but she kept on talking like I wasn't even there. (I've noticed that white people do this a lot.) Anyway, it wasn't long before I realized she was talking to Lucy Shields and she was talking about one of the ministers at their church. "What am I going to do, Lucy?" she said. "I feel so guilty. There he is, a priest of the gospel standing up there in front of everybody preaching about sin, and all I want to do is reach under that beautiful robe he wears." Well, as I said, I kept on going in and out, bringing in my stuff, but that's the kind of conversation you can't exactly ignore. And when I came in the next time with the vacuum cleaner, she was saying, "And I feel so guilty about Beaumont. I know I'm not being a good wife to him." And I decided I'd better go on upstairs and start cleaning the bedrooms.

When I came down later, Mrs. Archer seemed to have pulled herself together a little, and she said, "Braxton, are you interested in another job?"

"Well," I said, "this seems to be my big week for gettin' new jobs. What is it?"

"It's the job of sexton at our church."

"Oh."

"The old sexton is retiring, and we need to replace him."

"You mean it carries retirement benefits?"

"Yes, of course it does."

"Then I'd sure like to talk about it," I said. And suddenly the idea of workin' in a church where they paid retirement benefits and where people came to pray seemed a lot more attractive than workin' at an abortion clinic where people came to correct their mistakes and where other people tried to kill 'em for it. "What do I have to do?" I said.

"Well, I'm on the committee," Mrs. Archer said. "And Lucy Shields is, too. We'll have to set up a meeting for the committee to interview you."

"That would be fine with me."

"Do you go to church?"

"I go to Goshan Baptist Church," I said.

"Well, I don't think they'll hold that against you," she said. "This is an Episcopal church."

"Well, I won't hold that against them, either," I said.

She laughed at that, and then she promised to set up a meeting for me the following week, and I went on to see if I could catch my brother when he finished his last class over at John Marshall High School.

6

When I got to the school, the last busses were pulling out of the yard for the day, and I went on inside to see if I could find Billy in his classroom. He teaches math, and he was in the middle of trying to solve a problem when I walked in. Had all these numbers and symbols written across the blackboard like some foreign language. But he turned and called to me across the room the minute I walked through the door. "Hey, Braxton!" he said, and he dusted the chalk off his hands and met me in the middle of the room to give me a hug like he always does. "What's up?"

"Well, I thought maybe you and me could go somewhere and talk for a few minutes," I said.

"OK," he said. "Just let me get to the end of this problem. I've got to teach it soon, and I want to do it right." He went back to the board and started re-tracing the problem from the beginning. "I'm trying to discover the value of A," he said.

"The value of A?"

"Yeah. When I've got two unknowns."

"Sounds like the way I run my life," I told him. By this time, he was scratchin' away at the blackboard again like he hadn't even heard me, but I kept on talkin'. "Except you're solving for A, and I'm trying to solve how to do a decent day's work without gettin' killed or bein' fired."

"You in some kind of trouble?" he said.

"Naw, not yet. But I don't want to get that way," I told him. "That's what I want you and me to talk about."

"OK," he said. And then he came to the end of his problem, and he began to erase the board. It's funny about Billy. We're alike in a lot of ways, but when he gets to workin' a math problem, he just kind of goes into orbit, concentrating on it. And then he'll come back and concentrate on regular daily stuff in the same sort of way. "Where you want to go?" he said.

"I thought we might ride up to the donut shop.

"OK."

We went out to the parking lot and he drove us in his car, and of course, soon as we got our coffee, I told him about the guy with the butcher knife and about talkin' to Frank and all. "But now I need a gun," I said. "Last night, it was one guy with a knife. Next time it may be two or three, and the next ones after that may have guns to start with."

"I see what you mean," Billy said. "According to my kids, the easiest place to get a gun in Richmond is down town at 2nd and Marshall Streets anytime after midnight."

"Billy, I ain't gonna be walkin' around by myself at 2nd and Marshall after midnight."

"Or maybe at any of the convenience stores," Billy said. "Maybe at a 7-11 or a Fetchit Store out on Staples Mill Road. You can buy anything you want, if you hang around a convenience store long enough."

"So I've noticed," I told him. "But the question is, 'where do those guns come from?' If I buy a hot gun and it's traced back to some crime I didn't commit, I'm gonna have a hard time explaining that to a jury."

"The other thing is, I could buy you one at a gun store," Billy said.

"Would you do that?"

"Sure. I bought mine last year, so I know there's nothin' in my background check to stop me."

"Sounds good to me," I said. "Let's go." And as soon as we finished our coffee, we were on our way to Greentop Sporting Goods out in the county.

Let me tell you, that place was jumpin'. Here it was, late summer goin' into fall, with the days gettin' shorter and hunting season coming on, and Greentop was full. Some people were lookin' at fishing gear, of course, for the fall season, and some were lookin' at hunting rifles and shot-guns, but the biggest crowd was leaning over the glass top counters lookin' at pistols. I tell you, of all the mechanical devices ever invented, I believe a pistol grabs people's attention the most. They just can't look away from 'em. And that store carried everything from .22's to .44 magnums to .45 revolvers and automatics, even pistols that fired shotgun shells. Guns designed for every range and requirement. And the customers, men mostly but some women, were lined around those counters studyin' them guns the same way guys study the strippers in a topless bar, studying every curve and every goose bump and now and then saying something like, "sexy" or "trim," using one or two words, "too much," or "too heavy" or "just right."

Billy and I took our place in line, moving along the counter past the collector's items like Colt .44's and Lugers and P-38's and Pony Express Specials till we got to the secondhand guns where I saw one of the prettiest little automatic pistols I ever saw in my life. "Look at that one, Billy," I said. "It'd fit in my pocket without even a bulge."

"You want to see it?"

"Yeah, sure," I said.

So when the clerk finally got to us, Billy asked him to take it out and let us look at it. It was a Walthur double action .32, and although it was pretty expensive, it was priced at about half of what some of the new guns were sellin' for. Billy took it and cleared the chamber and handed it to me, and I tell you it was like fallin' in love. I'm not kiddin'. I remember the first time I fell in love when I was in high school. This gal walked into the classroom one day and just washed me away. And lookin' at that pistol made me feel the same way. It was so perfect. Balanced. Fitted in my hand like it was made for my hand. I aimed at a spot high up on the ceiling and squeezed the trigger. "Man! Billy, I got to have this gun," I said.

"You want to get it now?"

"Yeah, I want to get it now. See somethin' you like in this world, ain't no point in lookin' further, is it?"

"OK, give it here. You got the cash?"

"Yeah. I got the cash."

" I'm going to put it on my credit card," Billy said. "You can pay me when we get to the car."

"OK," I said. And then while Billy paid the clerk and the clerk got to runnin' the background check on the telephone, I backed out of the line to make room for the next customer.

That was when I first saw the man with snakeskin boots.

If it hadn't been for the boots, I doubt I would have even noticed the man at all. But I'd never seen nothin' like them boots. They looked so soft and easy, but at the same time, they looked really tough because they must have been made from rattlesnake skin with all that design and color that a rattlesnake has got. But then, it wasn't just the boots, either. The guy was wearin' these tight black britches and a black belt with a silver buckle and a blue stone at the center which I learned later was a piece of turquoise. What I'm get- tin' to is that this guy was not your typical resident of Hen- rico or Hanover County, Virginia. He wasn't white and he wasn't black and he sure wasn't like any of the local Indians I'd ever seen. The Pamunky and the Mattaponi Indians have kind of rounded and soft features, but this guy's face was sharp, and he had this carefully trimmed mustache. It wasn't until I heard him speak in Spanish to the guy next to him that I got the whole picture. He was a Mexican, but he wasn't like any Mexicans I'd ever seen, either. Not like the migrant farm workers that come through each summer or like that bunch that used to work up at Tyson's meat packing plant.

Most of those guys were short and looked either overweight or under-fed. But this guy was tall and trim, and he spoke to the man next to him like he was used to givin' orders. He was lookin' at a .9 millimeter Smith & Wesson when I first saw him. And even though I couldn't understand what he was saying, I could see that the man in front was buyin' the tall man a pistol, the same way Billy had just bought one for me.

Well, about this time, Billy finished the sale and bought a box of cartridges and a dozen paper targets and a little clip-on holster, and we walked out of the store into the parking lot. "I really appreciate you doin' this for me," I told him.

"Yeah, well. I don't want to read about 'em finding your body all hacked up in an alley because you had no way to defend yourself," he said. "But I want you to use it right. You hear me?"

"Yeah."

He waved the role of targets in his hand. "Sunday afternoon we're going out to the old farm and get in some target practice."

"Target practice?"

"Yeah. I hope you never have to use this gun, but if you do, I want you to come out on top."

"You're a good brother," I said. "Thanks." And then as he drove me back to my truck which was still parked at the school, I took that pistol out of the box and held it in my hand and looked at it, feeling its weight so evenly balanced.

And that night when I parked my truck in the alley and went to work at the Corporation with that little pistol clipped to my belt, I felt like I had a friend I could really count on.

7

But while a pistol makes a good defense against an enemy you can see, it ain't worth a damn against an enemy you can't see. And I learned that lesson in a big way two nights later when I went back to work down at the clinic.

On that night, from the minute when I drove into the parking lot, it seemed like things were different in some way. Even before I got out of the truck, I noticed that somebody had stacked three of them red bio-hazard bags outdoors beside the dumpster—a thing they had never done before. And then, inside the building when I was bagging the trash from the cans they had around the place, I felt something scratching against my leg and I looked down to see a used hypodermic needle stickin' through the side of the bag and into the leg of my pants.

Now, I knew they'd hired a couple of new nurses and a couple of new orderlies who worked in the daytime and that they might not be as careful as the regular staff, but this day and time, it doesn't take a medically trained person to know that one prick from an infected hypodermic needle can change your whole life. It didn't seem to have broken the skin, but it scared me, and I knew I was gonna have to talk to somebody about that stuff.

Anyway, I went on to finish my work—bein' extra

careful, of course—and I was busy runnin' my Hoover on the carpets upstairs when I started smellin' this funny odor. Smelled like kerosene or gasoline or something, and I shut off the vacuum cleaner and went downstairs to see what it might be. That's what saved my life, I guess, the odor and me going downstairs, because downstairs the odor was stronger than ever, and no sooner did I reach the bottom of the steps than there was this enormous Puff! and the whole waiting room area was suddenly filled with fire. Jesus! that was a scary sight. Thank God, it didn't explode big like it might have done if whoever set it had just waited a while longer. But that sort of thing really gets your attention! I picked up the phone and called 911 as I headed for the exit, and it wasn't more than three minutes before the fire crew was there and had the fire out in less time than it takes to tell about it. But it pretty well finished me for that night. The police came, and they all wanted to hear my version of the story. And then they found that somebody had bored holes in the side door and then poured kerosene inside and struck a match to it. As it happened, the kerosene had poured onto the slate floor instead of the wood floor, and whoever did it just hadn't poured in enough kerosene to do the whole job. But you see what I mean by unseen enemies.

 I never did get to the karate studio that night. It was near'bout 4:00 AM before I got finished talkin' to the police and the fire investigator, and I just went on home. Sadie woke up when I came in and I told her what happened. She just laid there for a minute, and then she said, "Braxton, are you gonna keep on workin' at that place till somebody kills you?"

And I said, "Naw, I hope not."

"Well, I think you should quit," she said. "Just quit."

"But, Sadie, we need the money."

"Not if you're dead, we don't."

"If we ever retire, we've got to save back enough to live on," I told her.

"But you've got to be living in order to enjoy it."

"Besides," I said. "I hate to run away from something."

"That's just silly, Braxton. It's dangerous down there."

"I keep rememberin' what my granddaddy did when that whole gang of men were givin' him a hard time for settling down with a black woman."

"That was different."

"He didn't run, I tell you. Took his shotgun out in the dark and fired up in the air and told them men to get off his place. And then when they got off a ways, he fired a load of number eight birdshot into the rear end of the horses and mules they were riding."

"That was a different time. And it was out in the country. This is in the city, and you can find another job," she said. "Livin' a long life without much money, is a lot better than bein' brave and letting some crazy fool kill you."

"OK," I said. "I'll think about it." And then I tried

to go to sleep, but it took a long time. It's really hard to get the picture out of your mind when you've seen a whole room full of fire.

But, as you can well imagine, I spent the next day like a squirrel runnin' around in a cage. First, I had to square things with Mr. Woo for not cleaning the karate studio after the fire, and then I had to talk to the police again and go over all the stuff I'd told 'em the night before. And then there were the newspaper reporters who were doing a big article on abortion services in Virginia. Last of all I had to talk to the people at the clinic and get some things straight about loose hypodermic needles and all. Even had to cancel my regular hours at Lucy Shields's house so I could do everything.

But as it turned out, the clinic wasn't badly damaged. They closed the place for a few days, and we all worked overtime trying to clean up the soot and get rid of the smell of fire and get some painters in to freshen up the place. But by the next week they were back doing business as usual—or maybe better than usual because Alice told me that following the fire, they went from doing twenty abortions a day to doing twenty-nine or thirty—which tells you something about how effective the pro-lifers are in tryin' to stop abortions. But I can tell you that the pro-lifers didn't quit. It won't more than a couple of days after the fire that I went home and found another call on my answering machine. This man's voice sounded like a preacher's voice sayin', "Did you smell the fire, Braxton? Did you get a good whiff? Well, you should remember it because that's what hell fire is going to smell like when you go there for working at that clinic." And then the son of a bitch hung up. But, oh my Lord, this kind of stuff begins to get to you after a while! Makes it really personal. They weren't just trying to burn down the clinic. They were tryin' to roast me!

Still, I didn't know what I could do about any of it, so I just did what I always did when things got troublesome: I went back to work and on that morning I went to work for another one of my daytime customers, Mr. Julius Seidell, who I haven't told you about yet.

Mr. Seidell is a lawyer, insurance man, and real estate dealer who has an office up on North Boulevard near Broad Street. He used to have a lot of people workin' in the office, until one day a couple of years back, he decided he wanted a new life. He closed out his insurance and real estate business and started remodeling the unused part of his office into one of the nicest apartments you ever saw. Then he divorced his wife, placed all sorts of annuities on his children, and moved into this new apartment, which of course, he also wanted me to clean along with his office. I usually just cleaned the place one day a week, unless he called me for something special, and like my other places, I had a key and could come in and work whenever I wanted.

Sometimes he was there and sometimes he wasn't, but on that particular morning, since nobody came to the door, and the place was so quiet, I figured he was in court or out playin' golf like he often did. So I went on into the apartment and started Hoovering away at the carpet in the living room, minding my own business, you know, when all of a sudden I noticed something out the corner of my eye, and turned to see the most beautiful Oriental woman I'd ever seen in my life. She was standing in the bedroom doorway, and she wasn't wearing a stitch of clothes. I mean nothing, absolutely buck naked. Just standing there staring in my direction. I say she was staring in my direction because she didn't seem to see me at all. Just stared like she was lookin' right through me. Then, she walked on through the living room and into the kitchen and started making tea just like I didn't exist. Made me feel kind of funny, you understand, so I kept on Hoovering the carpet just like she didn't exist, either, until a minute later she strolled back through the living room carrying two cups of tea and went back into the bedroom. "Well," I said to myself, "I guess Old Man Seidell is kickin' up his heels a little bit." But then it won't long before Mr. Seidell came out the bedroom himself, wearing a kind of heavy brocaded bathrobe and all covered with smiles, and he clapped me on the shoulder and said, "Braxton, you're some fine man. How long you been workin' for me?"

And I said, "About ten years."

And he said, "Yes, that's about right. And I guess you know me about as well as anybody—my business, my living arrangements. Now you've even seen my woman naked. And I don't know many men that well."

I couldn't tell where he was goin' with this. I've

seen white men smile when it didn't mean nothin' at all. But about then, he started laughing, which made me feel better. "You were cool as the old cucumber when Tami walked out here," he said. "You want another job?"

"Doin' what?" I said.

"Cleaning the Tiptop Club."

"The Tiptop Club?!"

"Yeah. After hours on weekends. Our janitor got himself into some bad trouble last week, and we need a new man."

Now, I'd heard of the Tiptop Club. Do Good organizations had been tryin' to shut it down for years because of what they called the exotic dancing that went on there. A strip joint, in other words. It was the kind of place that on weekends booked in women who had big reputations, you know, girls from around the country who had been featured in Playboy or who had once had center spreads in Penthouse and who were famous enough to make half the white men in South Richmond want to abandon their workshops and tool sheds and come see the goods in person. But I'd never been to the Tiptop Club, and I didn't know many black guys who had, and I told Mr. Seidell. "It always seemed to me kind of an iffy situation when black guys and rednecks start lookin' at the same naked white woman," I said.

"Well, you can come in after we close, if you want to," he said. "Or, if you want to see the show, just find a place and make yourself comfortable where you won't have to mingle with the customers," he told me. "I'm half owner of the place, and I can promise you won't have any problems. We've got the biggest bouncers you ever saw."

"I don't know," I told him. "If my wife found out I was workin' in a strip joint, she'd have my head."

"Don't tell her," Mr. Seidell said. "It's simple. You won't be working there except on weekends after 2:00 AM, anyway. And I promise we'll make it worth your time." Then he mentioned a figure that was near'bout what I earned workin' at the clinic for a whole week.

"Oh, my Lord!" I said. "I'm sure gonna have to consider it."

"Sure," Mr. Seidell said. "Consider it. But we need somebody soon. And we need somebody we can trust. You'd be perfect. Absolutely perfect." And then, as he turned and started to go back to Tami, he stopped and said, "Why don't you meet me here tonight between 1:30 and 2:00 and we can go down there. I'll introduce you around and you can get the feel of the place—so to speak," he said. And he was smiling when he said it.

Oh my God! Workin' in a strip joint. I agreed to meet him and go down there, but as I left Mr Seidell's place that day, I was givin' myself every kind of lecture I could think of. "Now, you be careful, Braxton," I said to myself, "you've already decided to hide it from Sadie. And when you start hidin' stuff, look out.

"But think of the money," I said.

"Um humn. Yeah. Money's good," I said. But you're a good Baptist boy, and this ain't your usual line of work.

"Remember the money," I said. "Think of the money. And besides, I'm just goin' down there tonight to look the place over. I may not take the job at all.

"Yeah," I said to myself, "sure you are."

But I tell you, it was right much on my mind when I went back to work at the clinic that afternoon. I got there a little earlier than usual, just before the place closed, and I was workin' in the front part of the building, hauling out the trash that was ready to go, when this young man came to the door and asked if he could speak to me.

Now, of course, with all the stuff that was goin' on, I was instantly suspicious...what the hell did he want with me? I wondered. And since it was daytime and I'd left my pistol locked in the truck, I felt kind of naked goin' out to meet a stranger without it. But he was a nice lookin' young guy—well dressed, light complexion about like mine, maybe nineteen or twenty years old, and his eyes looked clear, not like he was on sump'n. So I stepped out the door and said, "Yeah, what is it?"

And he said, "I've got a problem."

"You and everybody else around here," I said. "What kind of problem?"

"It's a girl," he said.

And I had to laugh at that because it seems to me sometimes that 'a girl' is really the main problem any man has ever got. "What about her?" I said.

He first looked down at his shoes like he didn't want to speak, but then he said, "She's pregnant."

"Oh," I said. And I stopped laughin'. "And I suppose you're the one that did it?"

"Yeah. But I want to see she gets the right care."

"Well, depending on the kind of 'right' care you want, this is the place," I told him. "You can talk to one of the nurses in there and she'll make an appointment."

"But nobody can know," he said. "She's young."

"How young?"

"Seventeen."

"So that can leave you open to a charge of statutory rape, if anybody wanted to push it."

"And she's white."

"Oh Jesus!" I said. "What's your name?"

He looked down again like he didn't want to tell me, but then he said, "Dennis. Dennis Rutlege."

"Oh yeah," I said. "Your daddy's a lawyer, ain't he?"

"Yes sir."

"I've seen his name in the paper."

"And I don't want him to know about it either."

"Is the girl here today?"

He looked over his shoulder at the shiny black Buick that was parked at the curb. "She's in the car," he said. "But she doesn't want to do it today."

"Well, you all have got to get some things straight," I told him. "But come here." And I took him inside and introduced him to Alice who explained to him how everything would be confidential and how payment had to be made by postal money order in advance and all the technical stuff he needed to know. She was real sweet to him. "How far along is she?" she asked him.

"About two months."

"Well, you'd better bring her in soon. When you want to schedule it?"

"I have to ask her," he said.

And that's when I butted in. "Listen," I told him, "you've got a young girl out there and she's scared. She ain't gonna be able to make the decision. You've got to make the decision. Give the nurse a date."

"OK," he said. "Next Friday. That's a week away. It'll give us time to arrange everything."

And then Alice said, "What's the patient's name?"

And you can imagine my surprise when he said, "Betsy Shields."

Oh My God! That thing stayed on my mind for the rest of the day almost as much as the question of whether or not I'd take the job at the Tiptop Club. I didn't go back outside with Dennis because I knew Betsy was in the car and I didn't want her to see me and worry about whether or not I'd tell her mama. But I knew I was getting more tied up with the Shields family than I ever wanted to be, even if they were kin to me. Still, I worried about Betsy. She was really a sweet girl, always huggin' my neck. And now she'd got herself in a fix with a young guy who wasn't about to say no to a good thing when he saw it.

Anyway, as a result of what had been happening at

the clinic, I had postponed a lot of other people, so since I still had a good bit of time left before I had to meet Mr. Seidell, I went straight on out to the karate studio on West Broad Street as soon as I could get away from the clinic that night. Now the karate studio is not hard to clean, but it covers a lot of space. It's sort of like a gymnasium with carpeted floors and not much furniture to be moved. But they bill themselves as a "Martial Arts" studio, and they are really into Oriental ways of fighting. Their main advertising gimmick is an arrangement of swords that they display in the large plate glass window at the front of the building. I'm sure it attracts a lot of young guys who're turned on by the idea of pokin' and stabbing people, but it's the first thing I move out of sight whenever I go into the place, 'cause I don't want some fool breakin' the glass and grabbin' those swords while I'm in there.

But everything stayed calm that night—at least until I finished my job and was gettin' ready to go meet Mr. Seidell. I had got my gear loaded back in the truck about 1:00 AM and was fixin' to leave when I heard this terrible ruckus in the lot behind the Mexican restaurant next door to where I was parked. Sounded like a pack of hounds closin' in for the kill. I checked to make sure my pistol was hooked safe in my belt, and then I looked over there through the hedge, and Man! These guys were tumbling out the side door of that Mexican restaurant surrounded by a gang of yelling men, and they were goin' at it hard, slugging each other with their fists at first, but then one of 'em tackled the other one, and for a minute they were just rolling around on the ground till all of a sudden, Click! One of 'em broke free and was standing there crouched with a four-inch switch blade in his hand, and the other guy was holding a bloody arm. I couldn't understand a word they were sayin' 'cause they were yelling at each other in Spanish, but I knew this had the makings of a very bad scene until this tall guy came out the door behind 'em and everything changed. He reached them just as the second guy pulled out his own switch blade. But the tall man didn't pay no mind to the second guy at all. He just walked up behind the first man's knife hand and with one motion swinging up from the waist he had that man by the throat. Near'bout lifted him off the ground and drove him back against the wall so hard I could hear his head pop hollow like a ripe melon against the bricks. Didn't make another sound. He just crumpled in a pile. That's when I saw who the tall man was. In the light of a passing car, I had no doubt that it was the man with the snakeskin boots that I'd seen buyin' a pistol at Greentop. Man, he was sump'n! Walked right up to a knife fighter and beat him with one motion of his arm!

The tall man gave some orders then, and some other guys picked up the knife fighter, threw him in the trunk of a car, and drove off. And all of a sudden, that parkin' lot was just as quiet as you please.

I was sweating, of course, not from the work I'd been doing but from the excitement of what I'd seen. But what was it, after all? What had I seen? I felt like it was something important, but I couldn't tell for sure whether I had witnessed a killing or a heroic act by the tall man who broke up a knife fight. I started to follow them and get their license number, but then I thought, Braxton, it's none of your business, and the less you know about it, the better. Stay out of it. I wouldn't find out how it ended until two or three days later when I saw in the newspaper that the Henrico police had found a dead Mexican with a broken neck beside a deserted road out in the country. And even then, it would be hard to tell what I'd seen, so I didn't tell anybody, either then or later. I didn't even tell Sadie because she gets so nervous about these things. But in any case, I didn't have a whole lot of time to sweat about it that night because I had to rush downtown to meet Mr. Seidell.

He was ready and waitin' in front of his apartment when I got there, and he asked me to ride with him in his Cadillac, but I begged off and told him I'd just follow him to the club in my truck so I could learn the way better. Course, my real reason was I wanted to be able to get the hell away from there on my own terms, if I had to, but I didn't tell him that. Anyway, we got down to the Tiptop Club just before closing time. Even then the parking lot was still full, and from the way the music was blarin' from the place, you'd think they were planning to go on for the rest of the night. "You sure they're gonna close?" I said.

"Oh yeah." he said. "It's the law. And before long, the cops will be around to make sure we conform to the law." About that time, we got to the door, which was outlined in red light, and I tell you, Mr. Seidell went in like visiting roy-alty. The big doorman bounced up off his stool the minute he saw us and rushed forward to shake Mr. Seidell's hand, and pretty soon, the other workers in the place were comin' over, both the men in their jackets and the women in their scanty little next to nothin' see through suits, and Mr. Seidell was treating them like they were all his children. He'd pat them on the back and give 'em a hug and ask about their families. He even hugged Boris, the big bouncer. And then he intro-duced me like an old buddy. "This is Braxton Bragg," he said. "He's an old friend, and I'm trying to persuade him to take Harry's place. So when he comes down here, treat him well, treat him nicely." They all shook hands with me, and then we walked on into the dining room.

I tell you, I've never seen such a place in my life. It was a restaurant, complete with tables and chairs and a full kitchen, because they served lunch and dinner six days a week, but in the middle of the dining room they had a large bar surrounded by this horseshoe shaped stage where the girls did their dance. And man! It was some dance they did! Just as we got there, the MC up in the sound and light booth was announcing that this was the last dance of the night, so everybody should welcome the beautiful TERESA! And all sorts of applause and shouts and whistles went up as Teresa came out and began to spin and gyrate and take off the few skimpy little things she had on. And I tell you, I never saw such a body in my life! I didn't know they made bodies like that, and as far as I could see, she wasn't wearin' a stitch.

'Course, when she came closer, I could see she did have a little flesh colored g-string over her crotch, and Mr. Seidell told me that if she showed even one pubic hair the cops would close the place down, but you can guess that the imagination had no trouble fillin' in the blanks.

Well, she whirled around and whirled around, teasing us with this kind of shawl she carried, and the guys around the bar were all reachin' up to stick dollar bills under the garter she wore on her thigh. Some of 'em were lucky enough to stick their bills inside her g-string. But then she saw Mr. Seidell and got all excited, waving to him and calling to him over the music. "Julius!" she said. "Julius!" And she came over to the edge of the stage and leaned down and hugged him. I mean that was somethin'! Teresa leaning over with her titties hangin' up against the front of Mr. Seidell's shirt while she hugged him. And damn if he didn't introduce me right there while she was huggin' him. "This is Braxton," he said. "He's going to work here." And she moved over and hugged me, too!

"Hello, Braxton," she said. "I'll be seeing you around." And she pulled my face right in between her titties as she stood up. Oh my God! I've never seen such a thing in all my life. And the other guys around the stage were all shoutin' and screamin' for her to do the same thing for them, when the MC's voice sounded out extra loud: "Thirty seconds gentlemen, thirty seconds. Keep your eyes open for the big show." And Teresa was up again, twistin' and turnin' and runnin' her thumbs inside the strap of her g-string and pullin' at it like she might be gonna jerk it off until just then the MC said, "Here it is! the whole story, gentlemen, NOW!" And she pulled it down just as the lights went out.

Well, I tell you the shouts and whistles that went up in that dark moment were enough to deafen you. When the lights came back on a second later, Teresa was gone, and if truth be known, it had all happened so fast, you couldn't really tell whether you had actually seen Teresa without her g-string or not. But she made you think you had, and I think her customers were satisfied.

"That's quite a show," I said.

And Mr. Seidell said, "Oh yes, we have our fun. That last moment's a little hard to time, but Teresa's got it down pretty close. Enough for us to stay legal, you understand." And then he pointed to the guy in the light booth. "Come on over and I'll introduce you to Jesus. He's the manager of the club."

For a second, I really didn't think I'd heard him right. "You'll introduce me to who?" I said.

"To Jesus," he said. And then he sort of laughed. His name's Jesus Romero. I think he's from Mexico, one of those Latin countries. Of course, down there they pronounce it Hesus, but up here, we all call him Jesus."

"You mean, if I go to work here, I'll be workin' for Jesus?"

"Well no, not exactly," he said. "I'm the boss, and you're my man. But Jesus is the club manager."

"Jesus shows up in some unexpected places, don't

he?" I said. And he laughed at that.

"You'll get along with him," he said. "He's managed clubs all over the East Coast. He know's what he's doing."

"Yeah," I said. "I'm sure he does."

And then by that time, Jesus was down from the light booth and on his way over to shake hands. He was a smooth talkin' man with just a little bit of Mexican accent, and he had this carefully shaped moustache that made him look sort of like a movie star, and I could guess pretty quick who was gettin' most of the action around the Tiptop Club after hours.

"Braxton, meet Jesus," Mr. Seidell said. It would take some gettin' used to. "Braxton is thinking about taking Harry's place," he said, "but he's worried that some of these rednecks down here might not like a black guy mixin' in with our girls."

"Don't you worry, my friend," Jesus said. "You'll be safe here."

"It ain't necessarily here that worries me," I said. "It's away from here."

"Still, we have our ways of dealing with trouble makers, I promise you," Jesus told me. "Trouble never lasts long and it's never caused by the same man twice. We take care of our people."

For some reason, I really felt like I could believe him.

"He's already met Boris," Mr. Seidell said.

"Oh yes. Boris will be your best friend in time of

trouble," Jesus said. "Come join us. I promise the work here is a lot of fun."

Well, between the two of 'em over the next ten minutes they persuaded me I should take the job, and I did. But I drove away feelin' kind of divided about it. I liked the money, but I haven't been a nigger in the South all my life and not learned a few things about reality. I figured I could handle myself OK, but I wasn't sure I could handle Teresa. And her huggin' up to me in front of a bunch of half drunk white guys at two o'clock in the morning had the makings of a really sad story.

And then there was the smell of Teresa's perfume that she'd left all over my face and neck. "Good God A'mighty!" I said as I got back in my truck. "I feel like I need a shower. If Sadie gets a whiff of this stuff, she'll kill me."

So instead of goin' straight home, I detoured by the clinic and went into the washroom where I could get myself cleaned up real good. But by the time I got my face dry, I had more questions than ever. Yeah, I was gonna take this job at the Tiptop Club, I thought. I'd be a fool not to, given the kind of money they were offering. But they wanted me to start right away, and how in the hell was I gonna do that with everything that was coming up? Remember that in addition to trying to make up the time I'd lost with my other customers while I was workin' overtime at the clinic, it was also the week that Lucy Shields wanted me to work at the Museum and the week I was supposed to interview for the job of sexton down at the Episcopal Church. So I already had my hands just about as full as they could be—or so I thought.

And then, the next day, I found out that Elva was coming home.

8

Elva. Oh My God! No matter what business I had at the Tiptop Club or the clinic, the Corporation or the church, Elva was right up there under the heading of Unfinished Business. I found out about it from my brother Billy when he called me just before his lunch break the next morning. "I don't want you to get into any trouble," he said, "but I talked to Ronnie McNight yesterday, and he told me his sister Elva's coming home from Chicago for a visit. Thought you'd like to know."

I think all I said for a minute was, "Oh my God!" And then I didn't say anything else for another minute.

"Braxton, you still there?"

"Yeah," I said. "I'm still here. I was thinkin'. I don't exactly know what I'll do about Elva comin' home, but thanks for tellin' me."

"Like I said, don't do anything stupid."

"I ain't gonna do nothin' stupid," I told him "When's she comin'?"

"Today. For special services at Emmanuel Church. She'll be here for the rest of the week."

"Oh shit!"

Now don't get me wrong. My wife Sadie is a good woman, and I love her. We've got a good marriage and I want to keep it, but Elva...! You remember what I said when

I bought that pistol, that seein' it was like falling in love for the first time? Well, Elva was the girl I was thinkin' about. Elva is (or was) the girl who walked into that high school history class on a September morning when I was sixteen years old and just washed me away. I'd never seen anything like her, and I guess I never have since, because for about four years after that, Elva was the most important person in my life.

You see, when I was sixteen, I didn't have no idea of nothin'. I was just another country boy, rockin' along, goin' to school, goin' home in the afternoon to help my daddy slop the hogs or feed the chickens, but I didn't have no idea of myself bein' a person in the world, of having a job, or makin' something of myself—until the day when Elva walked into that classroom. She was a light girl with this pretty hairdo. It wasn't an Afro, exactly, but it wasn't straightened, either. It was just pretty. And smart! God Almighty! She knew just about everything. The teacher sometimes had to quiet her down so some of the other kids could answer. Her daddy was the preacher at this big Baptist church a few miles from my house, so I guess she inherited some of his ability to talk in public.

I walked out of class with her that day and I spoke to her and she was nice. But it was the first time I'd ever felt timid around a girl. Always before, I'd been able to joke and cut the fool with almost any girl who walked by, but with Elva, I was afraid I'd say the wrong thing. And all of a sudden, I realized that I wasn't nothin' and that I had to be somethin' to make any kind of impression on Elva at all.

That was the first year our school had fielded a track team. We'd had football and basketball before, but ball games had never interested me specially. Track was something else. You might be part of a team, but you were always on your own to make your own mark, and I was suddenly hot for track. The coach sized me up for a runner right away—although I did the high jump and the javelin throw pretty well, too. But by the end of that year, I had placed first in the state in the 440-yard dash, second in the hundred, and second in the mile, and all of a sudden, I was somebody, or thought I was. When I wore my athletic sweater and walked out of class and down the hall with Elva, I felt I had a right to be with her. I had my name in the paper and my picture on the sports page. And she didn't miss this stuff, either. She showed every sign that she liked bein' with a state champion. I'd walk with her to the bus, and sometimes I'd walk all the way home with her to her house. Sometimes we'd take a short cut through the woods and fool around a little—nothin' serious, but enough to make a teenaged boy totally lose his mind. I even started goin' to church at her daddy's church, where she'd meet me and sit with me through the service. And of course, her daddy didn't miss this from up there in the pulpit. He was a tall man with a big loud voice and a way of gettin' almost everybody in the congregation to respond at once. He'd get the rhythm goin', and almost immediately the folks would start answerin', "Amen, Brother!" "Bless Jesus!" "Oh yes, Lord!" But in that year, I'd changed. And as a seventeen year old boy who was in love and who'd just won a state championship, I was feelin' frisky enough to cut the fool anywhere with anybody, even in church with Elva. And if I ever got around to sayin' Amen, it was because I was thinkin' of her. Oh yes, Lord! Let her be mine. Even with all the racket in church, I'd get restless sittin' there, and I'd be thinkin' how pretty Elva was and how good she tasted when I kissed her, and I'd let my hand slip over and rest up against her thigh—which she would remove without even lookin' down but with this half smile on her face like she was about to bust out laughin', and then maybe a minute later I'd let my hand creep over there again, Oh yes, Lord! And we'd keep up this game till the service was over—which seemed like forever.

But like I say, her daddy saw quite clearly what was goin' on, and one Sunday, after we'd been playin' this game for a couple of months, he was waiting for us at the church door. You know how preachers do, stand at the door after the service smiling and making everybody feel good for having communicated with the Lord and for having donated gener-ously from their hard earned wages. Well, he was there, like always, sweating and smiling and shaking hands, especially with the old ladies who had managed to save back some-thin'. Usually Elva and I just slipped around to the side door and went on out wherever we were goin'. But on this day, he saw us and turned back from the old lady he was talkin' to and said, "You two wait around. I want to talk to you."

Now, in case you've never known any tall black

preachers, let me tell you somethin'. They can be just as sweet and nice and kindly as you please as long as everything is goin' all right. But when things ain't goin' right, you better look out cause you're about to find out what the wrath of God is all about. I think that down deep they all see themselves as Moses comin' down from the mountain with the Ten Commandments in his hand, and they'd just as soon bash your brains out with those stone tablets as not.

Anyway, as soon as her daddy could get away from his congregation, he grabbed each one of us by the elbow and said, "Come here to my office," where he slammed the door, turned around and looked at me and said, "Just what do you think you're doing?"

"Sir?" I said.

"Have you no respect for the house of God?"

"Well, er...ah...yes...."

"Well, you don't act like it. I see what you're doing, sitting down there in the middle of the church with your hand on Elva's leg.... And you....!" He pointed to Elva. "You... why do you let him get away with it? You're the preacher's daughter. Everybody in the church is looking at you!"

Oh, my God! It was awful. He called us every kind of sinner and Jezebel in the book until finally he focused on me with that voice that sounded like Gabriel's trumpet and said, "I want you to go away and leave Elva alone!"

That, of course, made me kind of dizzy, and all of a sudden out of nowhere, I near'bout yelled at him and said, "I want to marry Elva!"

And he said, "What?!"

"I want to marry Elva," I said again.

"And what kind of work is it that you do?" he said.

"I work on the farm."

"And how much education have you got?"

"I go to high school."

"Then tell me this. How do you plan to keep a wife, workin' around the farm and going to high school when you're seventeen years old?"

And of course, after that, all I could do was look at my shoes until he said, "I want you to go away and leave Elva alone until maybe ten years from now after you have made something of yourself." And then, he grabbed my elbow again and pushed me right into the hall and closed the door.

Oh My God! It was a bad time. About a month later, he got another church job up in Philadelphia or New Jersey somewhere and moved completely out of the state and took Elva with him. And that was the end of that. Oh, we talked by telephone from time to time, and a few times over the years when she would come back to visit her family, I'd slip by to see her, but it never led to anything, and gradually we just drifted further apart. But still, Elva was the first girl I ever loved, and she always had a special place. So when Billy told me she was comin' back to Richmond for a visit, I wanted to see her—even if it was one of the busiest weeks of my life.

Lucy Shields called me on Sunday afternoon right

after I got back from church with Sadie, and Lucy was full of herself, so excited and talkin' so fast she could hardly get all her words out. "Braxton, you're still planning to help us at the Museum, aren't you?" she said. And I told her that oh, yes, I was lookin' forward to it. And she said she wanted me to meet her at the Museum the next day to plan the whole thing. So I knew I was in for a long busy week. I told Sadie I'd probably not even see her till about the following Sunday—which would probably be the first time I'd get any sleep that week, also. But I've had long work weeks before, and if the pay is right, I can put up with just about anything.

So I met Lucy at the Museum about ten o'clock the next morning, along with a bunch of other folks who were planning this shindig, and I tell you, the place was jumpin' somethin' awful. This party was going to be so big that they couldn't even house it all inside the building. And when I got there, at least two tree removal companies were busy taking down three oak trees in the parking lot to make room for this big circus tent they were gonna put up to form an outdoor dining room. At the same time, inside the Museum, the decorators were hard at work tryin' to make the place look like Russia in the nineteenth century. I mean, that building's got a lot of marble and open space in it, but they had already decorated the front part to look like a Russian forest, and as you walked on inside, you came into The Imperial Hall of Mirrors and then into this blood red room that Lucy told me was supposed to be like the "Revolutionary Room," whatever that was. It all seemed sort of strange to me, since only a few years earlier we'd been about to go to war with Russia every time we turned around, but here we were decorating the showiest building in the old Confederate Capital to make it look like Russia under the Tsars and all to show off a bunch of fancy Easter eggs, made for somebody who had more money than brains. But I never did know nothin' about art no way, and since the pay was good, I figured they could do anything they wanted to do.

Anyway, just after I got inside, I saw Lucy standin' in the Marble Hall talkin' to a bunch of official lookin' people, some men, but mostly very polite lookin', gray haired Southern ladies. Now I don't mean anything bad about this, but I learned a long time ago that in this town, the real power and money is with the gray haired Southern ladies, and if you manage to get on their good side, then you've got it pretty well made.

Lucy saw me about the time I got to the middle of the room, and she turned to the others and said in that bouncy way of hers, "Here comes the man who's gonna keep this place spotless!" And she introduced me to the whole bunch of 'em. Well, what she wanted me to do was direct the temporary cleaning crew. The regular staff was too small to handle the job, but she had already hired three people and she wanted me to hire three more that would be responsible for setting up the tables and chairs and cleaning up after the decorators and running a kind of clean up patrol during the banquet and takin' out the trash from the kitchen and the dining area as fast as it built up. "And you have to be especially

careful on these marble floors," she said. "Because if something gets spilt and somebody slips and falls, we're going to
have the very devil to pay." I figured as how I could take care
of it pretty well, and I had already figured who I could hire
to help me by the time she finished showin' me the layout.
"And we want you to wear black pants and white shirts—or
black skirts and white blouses, if you hire women."

"OK," I said.

"This is a very visual party," she told me. "People
will be here to see things and to see people. I mean, we're
going to have the most famous people in the art world here.
So how you look is a very important thing."

"I'll take care of it," I said.

"I know I can count on you, Braxton. And if you need
extra equipment or anything to do the job, just let me know
and I'll give you the money to buy it. It's going to be beautiful, Braxton!"

"I'll get back with you," I said. But while she was
tellin' me all this stuff, I couldn't help thinkin' that on the
same day Lucy Shields was runnin' this great big party at the
Museum, her daughter Betsy was scheduled for an abortion
a few blocks away. But of course, that was none of my business, either. So I just went on like I didn't know nothin' and
did the rest of my work for the day.

9

Now, in my business, doing the rest of my work for the day is not so easy as it sounds. Remember that several of the places I had to clean were right there near the Museum on North Boulevard—lawyers' offices, a real estate office, a car dealership, in addition to Mr. Seidell's office and the clinic that wasn't far away. But remember also, if you will, that starting in the 1990s, North Boulevard was becoming a shooting gallery in every sense of that word. Since the police had been cracking down on the hookers and the pimps and the drug pushers that used to operate downtown, the hookers and the pimps and the drug pushers had moved their center of operation farther west on Broad Street to the intersection with North Boulevard. (Of course, moving west helped 'em, too, I suppose, since their customers from the nice houses in the West End didn't have to go so far to get what they wanted.) But the nearby area along North Boulevard was specially useful to 'em, too, because there was so much open dark space, park areas with secluded spots and trees and parking lots. All that shadow and half-light made a great place for the dealers to deal and for the users to use and for the hookers to take their customers for a quickie.

But that area became dangerous as hell after dark, except right around the Museum when they had some night function and had armed guards patrolling the place. But at other times, especially after midnight—well, forget it. The users would do anything, absolutely anything to get money for another dose of cocaine or crack or whatever it was. That summer they'd even killed the old crippled black man that used to sell flowers down there at the corner of Grove Avenue. Turned over his flower stall, knocked him in the head, and took his cash box. Poor old guy, never did nothin' in his life worse than grow pretty flowers and sell 'em on the street, but they got him. And lone women, well they were like walkin' targets, not for rape so much, although that did happen, but as possible sources of easy money or jewelry.

That was the year they killed five middle aged or elderly women within about a block of the Boulevard, and not all of 'em were killed on the street. At least three of 'em were in their own apartments. I knew one of 'em. Her name was Lizzie, white woman, must have been about sixty-five years old, and she had been walkin' around the Fan at night for years with her little dog named Rufus. I'd see her up there at the White Tower on Broad Street when I'd go in for coffee after cleaning the Oldsmobile show room or the Barton and Bocock law offices that were just off Broad Street. I'd see Lizzie at the counter and I said to her one night that I was surprised they let her bring her dog into a eatin' place.

And she said, "Oh, they know me here. And Rufus is a good dog. That's why I keep comin' back, 'cause they don't discriminate." And Rufus would just sit there beside her and wag his tail.

Well, I'd see her and Rufus all over town at all hours.

Sometimes I'd come out of the clinic about two o'clock in the morning and there would be Lizzie and Rufus strolling along like a couple of kids goin' to a picnic. And one night I said to her, "Lizzie, you know the streets are gettin' dangerous. I'm not sure it's safe for you to be walkin' around in all these places you go."

And she said, "Let me show you something." And she unzipped this big purse she always carried with her and pulled out the damndest lookin' hatchet you've ever seen. Sharp? That thing was like a razor. "Anybody bother me, he's gonna pull back a nub," she said.

"I see what you mean," I told her. And then after a minute or so, I said, "But suppose there's more than one of 'em, Lizzie. Suppose one of 'em grabs you from behind while you're whackin' away at the one in front."

She said, "Well, I've lived in this city all my life. It's a beautiful city. I got married here and I had my children here. And I'm not going to be driven from the streets by the hoodlums."

"OK," I told her, "but be careful."

Well, as it turned out, they didn't drive her from the streets, but they did kill her. Just like I told her, a couple of these worthless pieces of shit followed her to her house one night, back to where she lived in one of those big ramshackle houses on Monument Avenue, and they grabbed her just as she got the front door open. Killed her with her own hatchet. Killed Rufus, too. Then they took her purse and went on inside the house and took whatever else they thought they could sell or trade to make money for their next fix. Paper said she was the widow of one of the richest stockbrokers in Richmond and worth about five million dollars, but you'd never know it from lookin' at her. Just a sweet, sort of crazy old lady walkin' through the streets of the Fan.

But I was thinkin' about Lizzy that night after I talked to Lucy Shields at the Museum, wondering if they had enough armed guards to protect the rich folks who'd be comin' to the party. It had been a long day when I finished cleaning the Barton and Bocock offices about 2:00 AM, and I was tired something awful. But I was still being careful when I came out the door, you know, watchin' my back like I always do. There weren't many people on the street on Monday night, since I guess most of the hookers were restin' up from the weekend. But of course, the drug business never stops. And once my eyes got used to the dark, I could see these guys waiting in a doorway or just standing in the shadows along the side of a building.

Anyway, as I started my truck, I saw the yellow warning light on the dash telling me I was just about out of gas, so a couple of minutes later, I pulled into the service station and convenience store up on the corner of Broad Street. Now this place has always been kind of lively. It's one of the few places downtown that stay open all night, so all the night people tend to show up there sooner or later, no matter whether they're hookers or high school students comin' home from the senior prom. That place and the twenty-four hour drug store across the street are sort of the real crossroads of Richmond. If you ain't seen it before, you just go up to one of them places and wait for a while after midnight, and I promise that sooner or later you'll see it, whatever it is.

Anyway, I pumped myself a tank of gas and went in to pay for it. And the first thing I saw as I came in the door was the man in snakeskin boots comin' out of the men's room. Sort of gave me a chill when I saw him, strollin' out of that men's room like he owned the whole damn store, the same cool dude he'd been before when I saw him back of the Mexican restaurant. He motioned to three other guys who were playin' a video game in the back of the store. And them other guys just snapped around like soldiers and followed him out. You've sort of got to admire a guy that's got that kind of control over people. I watched 'em walk out and get into a big Lincoln Continental, and then I paid my bill and went into the men's room myself.

Oh My God!

If they'd wanted the place painted red, they couldn't have had a more complete job because that toilet was simply awash with blood. I thought I'd seen some hard things in my time, but when I opened that door I near'bout threw up right on the spot. Not only was the room filled with the hot and salty-sweet smell of fresh blood, but there was a man layin' on the floor with his head in the commode.

Now, your first instinct is to pull the man out of the commode, but I seen right away there won't no use doin' it because his throat had been cut from jaw to jaw and his blood was now pouring into the water. Jesus! What a sight! I just backed out and stood there till I got hold of myself, and then I walked out to my truck and drove off.

Oh Lord! I think I must have been driving strictly by habit, on automatic, because I couldn't think of anything but what I'd seen in that men's room. Like the sight of the fire in the clinic, the sight of that bloody room just pushed everything else out of my mind. I had a truck load of trash that I needed to take out to the dump, and somehow I got it there. But I don't remember drivin' at all. I was just suddenly there. That's when I began to come around, hearing them trash bags, concealed bio-hazard bags and all, bump up against each other at the county dump as I threw 'em in. Oh God! I remember thinkin', what are we comin' to, after all? Cut a man's throat and stick his head in the toilet! How could somebody do that sort of thing? And then, I was thinkin', even worse, how could I just walk away and leave him there? But what should I have done, anything? I obviously wasn't going to save his life. All I would have done was to get myself involved with something really nasty. And who in the hell needs that? But I did feel bad for him, whoever he was, and I was sorry I couldn't help him.

10

The newspapers that week didn't even begin to describe the scene of the killin'. They just reported that the body of an unidentified man had been found in the men's room of a downtown service station and that there were knife wounds on the body. But then they said that the real cause of death had not yet been fully determined, which was a mystery to me, having seen him bleeding his life into the toilet bowl that night. It was like they didn't really want to deal with it. The whole report won't but about two inches long. But it seemed like to me that it was somethin' that should have set off alarms all over town. 'Course, that might have just been my way of lookin' at it in the light of all the other stuff that was happening, because before that week was over, I came to think of it as my "Red Week," maybe even my "blood week." It was a week that things began to change in me, and I started hoping, Tiptop Club or not, that the sexton's job at the Episcopal Church would work out so I could change the way I ran my life.

On Tuesday night when I got to the clinic, things seemed pretty quiet. And I guess they were quiet in a way, except that as soon as my headlights hit the area around the dumpster, I realized that another scourge of city living had struck—street people and junk collectors. You may not see so many of them during the day, but after dark the street people come out and start going down the alleys lookin' into trash cans and opening trash bags and half the time cuttin' the bags open and dumpin' the trash on the ground to see what's at the bottom. Lord! It looked like a hurricane had hit the yard behind the clinic.

Now the outside was not really my responsibility, but you know I couldn't go off and leave the place lookin' like a landfill, so I got my shovel and rake out the bed of the truck and started tryin' to pull that stuff together before the wind scattered it. That's when it happened. It had been a hot September day, and of course, the whole area smelled like the wrath of God to start with, and hurrying to get finished, moving around in the half-light from the street and with nothing more than the flashlight hooked to my belt, I stepped backwards into the dark at the corner of the dumpster and felt something sticky and squishy under my foot. That's when I stopped and shined the light down at my feet and saw that I had stepped right into the middle of one of them red bio-hazard bags filled with blood and fetuses. It was a bag the street people had cut open, and they must have had one hell of a surprise—human blood and decaying human tissue cooked in the sun on a hot September day. It covered my left shoe. And that time I did vomit. Right there in the yard. I just couldn't hold it back.

Blood and fetuses! Great God Almighty!

As long as that stuff was neatly closed up in thick plastic bags, it was just trash for me to haul to the dump. But that night I saw exactly what it was that I was hauling. And while most of that 'debris' comes out lookin' just like blood, a lot of them women must have had late term abortions because there were identifiable human parts in there. Little, teenie parts, but parts, all the same. Oh, My God! I was in the business of transporting human body parts to the dump!

Now, needless to say, this gave me a hell of a lot to think about that night and on afterward. Here I was providing a service and maybe doin' some good in the process by helping keep the city clean, but haulin' body parts! Was it even legal? I wondered. Suppose I was doing something illegal without even knowin' it and got caught for it.

I finally got it all cleaned up and found a bucket to throw water on the stained areas and try to wash the stains toward the gutter. I even poured a big bucket of water over my shoes trying to get 'em clean. But it's damn hard to get rid of the smell of decayed flesh and harder still to forget the sight of your own feet covered with blood, so after I finished throwin' everything else in the dump that night, I threw my shoes in there, too. Just didn't want to touch 'em anymore. Went home barefooted.

But that's when I really began to add things up. Sadie was asleep when I got in that night, but I woke up early enough the next morning to catch her before she went to work and found out where her calculator was.

"Why you need a calculator?" she said.

"Oh, I got a few things to add up," I told her. "You know, I'm workin' eight or ten jobs and sometimes I lose track of what's what." I didn't tell her about steppin' in the fetuses. What was she gonna do about it besides get all upset? So I just let her go off thinkin' I was gonna add up the money I was gettin' so I could keep the account books straight. But it wasn't money I wanted to figure, and as soon as she was gone, I got the calculator off the dresser and started doin' the numbers:

The clinic was, on average, performing 30 abortions a day and they were open six days a week. Click, click. That's 180 abortions a week. Now, they're open all year except for a week at Christmas and a week for the Fourth of July, so click, click, that's 50 times 180 which equals....Great God Almighty!...9,000 abortions a year. And I had been working for 'em for eleven years, so that's 99,000 abortions, ninety-nine thousand fetuses that I had personally hauled off to the dump. Jesus! It made my skin crawl. That's near'bout half the entire population of Richmond from that one clinic. And I knew there were at least two other full-time working clinics in town—one on Northside and one on Southside. If they were gettin' the same number of patients...oh, My God, I thought, if all those pregnancies had been carried to term, Richmond would be over twice the size it is!

How was I gonna think about this? I thought I was in the janitorial and house cleaning business, but here I was being an undertaker and didn't even know it. Was this sort of thing true in other cities all across the United States? I wondered. If it hadn't been for abortions, would the population of the entire country have doubled in the last ten years?

Well, of course, all this was more than I could answer

layin' there in bed on a Wednesday morning. And I didn't really have a whole lot of time to think about it because the phone rang, and it was my brother Billy calling on his break between classes. "Two things," he said. "First, what time do you want my boys over at the Museum this afternoon?"

I'd hired his two teenage sons to work with me for the Museum job, and I'd forgot about it. "Oh My Lord," I said. "I meant to call you, but I didn't get in till late last night. Can they meet me at the Museum about four o'clock? We've got to start settin' them tables up."

"I'll tell 'em," Billy said. "They're looking forward to it because it's more money than they've ever earned at any one job."

"They're good boys," I said. "But I'll need one other person."

"I've got a senior in my home room," Billy said. "A girl named Clarice. She's got a mouth on her, but she's smart. I think she'll do a good job, if she's interested."

"OK," I said. "Send her on with Ronnie and Philip. And thanks, Billy. You're a big help."

"One other thing," Billy said. "They're having a dinner and prayer meeting over at Emmanuel Baptist Church tonight, specially for Elva and her family. Her father's going to be there to preach the service."

"Oh My God! How am I gonna arrange that?"

"Well, I can't figure that one out for you," Billy said, "but that's where she's going to be, if you want to see her, about seven o'clock."

"I'll do my best," I said. And then I hung up and headed to the shower.

That day, starting in the afternoon, was going to be my first workday preparing the Museum for the big party. The out of order trees had already been cut down and hauled away, and the big circus tent had been erected in the yard, and it was going to be our job to make this outside space really suitable for a plush party where a lot of the guests would be millionaires. Of course, half the guests would be eating inside the building, but the outside part needed to be just as good and was gonna require the most work.

It was also a day when my other jobs were still in place, and the first one I had to go to was to the Shields's house to give it its mid-week cleaning.

Nobody answered the door when I got there, so I just let myself in with the key Lucy had given me and started with the downstairs, cleaning the kitchen and living room and library and all. And then as I picked up my vacuum cleaner and turned to go upstairs, I looked up and there was Betsy, dressed in next to nothin' standing at the top of the steps. Looked like she might have been sleepin'. "Braxton!" she said, "I didn't know it was your day to come." And she gave me the sweetest smile and came paddin' barefooted down the stairs and hugged my neck like she always did.

"Look out, now," I told her. "Don't hurt yourself on the vacuum cleaner," which I was holding as a kind of defense between her and me. And then, as she worked her way around the vacuum cleaner, I looked up and realized she was not alone. Dennis was standing at the top of the stairs. "I see you got company," I said.

And nonchalant as you please, she pointed and said, "That's Dennis. He's my friend from school."

"Yes," I said. "Seems to me like I've met Dennis somewhere before." He looked embarrassed, but he nodded and came on down the stairs, and I guess I should have kept my mouth shut, but I didn't. I just looked at him and looked at her and said, "I'm glad you're both in school because I think you've got a lot to learn."

"Braxton," Betsy said, "You won't tell Mamma that Dennis was here, will you?"

"I'm here to help your mamma," I told her. "I don't think telling her about Dennis is gonna help her very much at all." And then I pushed on around her and up the stairs.

That girl! Jesus! Don't nobody have any sense anymore? There she was, going for an abortion on Friday and doin' the same stuff on Wednesday that got her pregnant in the first place. I guess maybe she thought that one more toss in the hay wasn't gonna do any harm, considering the circumstances. But the whole thing just put me in a bad mood as I headed toward the Museum where I was gonna meet her mamma and all the other society folks that were putting on this shindig—the Faberge Ball.

I found Ronnie and Philip and Clarice waitin' for me beside the door like I told 'em. Clarice was a pretty little girl, but I could see right off from the way Ronnie and Philip were cuttin' the fool with her that they were all gonna need close supervision for this job. So I told 'em to calm down and told 'em what we were going to have to do, and then we went inside.

Lucy Shields was there with her husband, who is on the Board, if you remember, along with all the other board members. And they started off with Lucy introducing the people who were actually going to be running the show. First, there was Mr. Rodger Hopgood, a British guy that had been brought all the way from London, England, to design this party. And he was some fancy Englishman. You could just look at his clothes and tell he was an Englishman. His suit was crisp and trim and lean, something different from what most American guys wear, and he had a diamond stickpin at his collar and a pair of cuff links that flashed the light every time he moved. Mr. Hopgood said a few very crisp British words, and then he took over and began to introduce other people. And the first thing I noticed was that, except for the board and the cleaning staff, near'bout everybody had been brought in from somewhere else. The orchestra was coming down from New York; the food service company was coming from Washington where they catered banquets at the White House; the chef was a German; the waiters were Mexican and couldn't even speak English, and on and on. It's like they couldn't find nothin' in Richmond except somebody to clean up the mess. That's a thing I've noticed about Richmonders time after time: unless it comes from somewhere else, it ain't any good, which always seemed funny to me, considering the stuck-up airs that Richmonders like to put on.

But anyway, after all these preliminaries, we finally got to work doin' sump'n and went on into the early part of the evening, workin' in the tent and settin' up tables until I realized it was near'bout seven o'clock and if I was gonna have the slightest chance of seein' Elva, I was gonna have to get out of there. I called Ronnie and Philip and Clarice and told 'em what to do while I went off to "check on another job," and then I near'bout ran to my truck and took off for the Emmanuel Baptist Church. I hated that I didn't have time to shower and put on some fancier clothes, but there I was, running across town, exceeding the speed limit whenever I thought I could get away with it, and all the while, thinkin' of Elva on the other end. And I tell you I was some nervous fucker. What would she do when she saw me? Would she even recognize me? Would I recognize her? I mean, it had been years, after all. And would she want to talk to me, even if she did recognize me, specially with her daddy there? That damn stuck up son of a bitch—what would he say to me now?

I was a little late and the congregation was all gathered in the dining room and eatin' supper when I got there, but I managed to slip in at the tail end of the line and get a plate of food and find a seat, and then I looked around. I wasn't really a member of this church, but I knew a bunch of the people, had grown up with 'em, and they remembered me from high school days. I waved to several guys I knew and at my brother Billy who was on the other side of the room, and then up in front, I found the head table. I recognized Elva's daddy first. He hadn't changed much except his hair was white. And then there was her mamma, and last of all, at the end of the table there was Elva with some light dude sittin' beside her. She had put on some weight over the years, but it didn't hurt her none. She was still mighty pretty. I tried to catch her eye, but of course, she couldn't see me way at the back of the room, and then the preacher got up and announced it was time to move into the sanctuary of the church for the Wednesday night hymn singing which Elva was gonna lead. I had thought there would be more time before they went in, more of a quiet few minutes when I could just walk up and say hello without it bein' such a big deal. But now my time was runnin' out, and I had to get back to the Museum, and I knew that if I didn't get to see Elva soon, this whole trip was gonna be a big waste of time.

I slipped out the back door of that dining room with the idea that I could hurry to get in front of the others and catch up with her. But there was a middle door up front that I hadn't seen, and a whole bunch of folks were already in the hall between her and me. I could see her up front beside her daddy heading toward the sanctuary, and I almost called to her. But I stopped myself because I didn't think that was a good way to meet somebody you hadn't even talked to in so many years. So I pushed my way on through the crowd just far enough forward to see Elva go into the church, but by the time I actually got to the door, she was already on the stage playing the chords of the first hymn on the piano. Jesus! that made me feel weak. I wanted to run right up there beside her, but I knew I'd look like a fool. And then I turned around and saw my brother Billy behind me. I pulled him over to one side and said, "Billy, listen, I'm in real trouble here. I can't get in there to see Elva right now, and I've got to get back to the Museum to get the boys and Clarice." About that time the music started for real, and I looked over my shoulder to see that the light dude who'd been sitting at the table was standing up at the microphone beside Elva and singing "Nearer My God to Thee" in a high, kind of sweetish voice that made me want to puke. "What can I do, Billy?" I said. "Is there any way you can think of to get her out here for a minute?"

"Not for the next hour," Billy said.

"Well, can you at least tell her I came to see her and that I'm gonna call her at her brother's house?"

"Yeah, I can do that," Billy said. "You want me to give her your number?"

"Lord, no!" I told him. "You want to get me killed? Sadie would go up the wall if Elva called me at home. Just tell her I'm gonna call her tomorrow."

"OK," Billy said. "But if that won't work, you'll still have another chance to see her here on Friday because they're having a big revival meeting then."

"How can I do that?" I said. "I've got the Museum on Friday. Just tell her I'll call. We'll work something out." And then, I turned and ran down the hall and back to my truck.

11

I got back to the Museum in plenty of time to look over what we had done and to get the kids back home. And then, feeling really pissed off at near'bout everything in the world, I settled down to do the rest of my night's work: the clinic, the karate studio, and the car dealership out on Staples Mill Road. Everything was pretty quiet that night, thank God, except that when I got to the clinic, I found a box of clean hypodermic needles, along with an unopened shipment of drugs, layin' out on the back steps. What the hell was this? I thought. I knew they couldn't keep equipment like needles and certain medicines on the shelf for longer than just a few weeks. But in the middle of the Boulevard shooting gallery, to lay them needles and drugs on the back steps like a box of "free kittens" seemed to me to be stretchin' generosity a little far.

Anyway, I put the needles and all in a trash bag and got the place cleaned up and went on to the other places and worked to near'bout four o'clock before I managed to get home and fall in bed. And even then I didn't get but about three hours' sleep before Sadie woke me up gettin' ready for work.

"They called from the church," she told me. "They

want you there for an interview at eleven o'clock this morning."

"OK," I said. "I hope I don't fall asleep in the middle of it."

And then Sadie said, "And on the way downtown, stop by the post office and get some stamps and mail these bills I just paid."

She dropped a handful of envelopes on the dresser and left, and I thought I was going to roll over and go back to sleep, but all of a sudden I was wide awake, thinkin' first of calling Elva and what I was going to say to her and then about meeting with the committee at the church and what I was going to say to them. And little did I realize that on that day, of all the things I had to do, going to the post office would be the most important.

I did try to call Elva before I left, tried about four times, in fact, each time planning in my mind what I was gonna say so I wouldn't sound too stupid, dialing the number and waiting, and then finding the line was busy. Each time! Made me feel like throwin' sump'n. You know how it is. You're nervous anyway, and you're reachin' out, but all you get is buzz, buzz, buzz.

Anyhow, I finally gave up for the morning and got dressed. And of course, on that day, since I was going down for an interview at the church, I dressed especially well—puttin' on my dark blue Sunday suit and a white shirt and a gold necktie—just by way of lettin' the Episcopalians know that they would have a man of quality doin' their scut work for 'em— especially when it came to helpin' the elderly gray haired ladies out of their cars in front of the church on Sunday morning. Then I headed down to the post office, bitchin' and moanin' the whole way over the fact that I had to go inside for stamps instead of just droppin' the bills in the street box.

So I parked and went in, and of course, had to stand in line. Seemed like the clerks were workin' mighty slow that morning, so I stood and waited and fidgeted and read all the signs on the wall, and then, about three people back from the counter, I came up beside the FBI bulletin board of "most wanted" criminals, which I also read. There were some white guys among 'em, but most of 'em were black, and I read the description and history of each one until I got to the middle of the bottom row, where I stopped in total cold surprise. It was the man in snakeskin boots lookin' back at me. Oh my God! The man with snakeskin boots! His name was Alphonso Ramirez, and he was wanted in Texas on a fugitive warrant for smuggling, drug dealing, money laundering, and the murder of five people—for which he had already been convicted before escaping from that Texas jail. Alphonso Ramirez. And not the least thing on that flyer was the big note at the bottom: $20,000 DOLLAR REWARD TO ANYONE PROVIDING INFORMATION LEADING TO THE ARREST OF THIS FUGITIVE. HE IS KNOWN TO BE ARMED AND THOUGHT TO BE EXTREMELY DANGEROUS. And then they gave the telephone number to call.

I tell you, seein' that poster made my heart beat even faster than it had on the night when that dude pulled the butcher knife on me. Twenty thousand dollars!

He was a damn gold mine!

And I'd been seein' him all over town!

I waited till I was pretty sure nobody was lookin', and then I jerked the poster off the bulletin board and stuck it in my pocket and walked on up to the counter smiling as nice as you please to get my stamps.

Alphonso Ramirez.

Also known as: Al Ramirez, Alli Ramirez, Alli Rama, and Sergio Ramirez. And of course, I still thought of him as Snakeskin.

Well, whatever his name was, I knew he wasn't far away, and by the time I had stuck my stamps onto them envelopes and walked out to the front steps of the post office that morning, I just knew that Alphonso Ramirez, the man with snakeskin boots, both him and that twenty thousand dollars were gonna be mine, one way or another. That was gonna be the thing, I thought. That would be the key to changing my life in a big way.

Now, this sort of thing does something to you, makes you more alert, even if you were alert before. It makes you conscious of everything, makes you see more. I knew Ramirez drove around in a Lincoln Continental, so I was alert to every Continental on the highway. I knew he got gas at the corner of Boulevard and Broad, so I checked that station and others along Broad Street. I knew he liked to eat at the Mexican restaurant near the karate studio, and even before I went for my interview at the church, I circled out there and drove around the restaurant just in case I might see his Lincoln in the parking lot. I swept the street with my eyes, checking out every Mexican who walked by. And of course, I thought of Jesus down at the Tiptop Club, wondering if he might know anything about other Mexicans in town.

So with all these thoughts of wild Mexicans and big bucks running through my mind, along with occasional thoughts of how I was gonna hook up with Elva, I finally parked in front of the Episcopal church, warned myself to be calm, and went inside for my interview just before eleven o'clock.

Of course, when I first walked into the church on that weekday morning there wasn't a soul in sight, so I looked around a little bit. In the vestibule, (later I would learn to call it the "Narthex," but to me it's still a vestibule) I saw all these brass placards on the wall commemorating the visits of famous people, people like President Jefferson Davis and Governor Harry Byrd and President Franklin D. Roosevelt, but mainly they were about the visits of Confederate generals...General Robert E. Lee, General A.P. Hill, General Benjamin Nelson, and last—over on the side—they had one to General Braxton Bragg. He had been there in 1865, just before Richmond was burned. "Uh huh," I said to myself, "this seems to be my kind of place. Good to know the old boy went to church." And then I went on into the main sanctuary with its odor of old books and dust and the light from the morning sun shining through a stain glass window to make a red patch across the pews and along the main aisle. It was a nice old building, but I could tell right away that the people who ran it were pretty persnickety from the way the books were arranged in the racks along the backs of the pews. Looked like soldiers all lined up at attention—a red hymnal and a black prayer book, alternating one after the other. Must have taken somebody half a day to line up all them books—but it gave me an idea about the folks I'd be dealing with. And then I heard my name called, and I looked around to see Mrs. Archer standing in the doorway. "Braxton," she said. "I thought you'd gotten lost. We're next door in the meeting hall."

So I followed her along through the hallway to the meeting place where she introduced me to the others on her committee. There was the Reverend David Mann, the assistant rector, and Mrs. Alice Crabbe, and Mr. Ogdan Huffines, the senior warden, along with Mrs. Archer, of course. "Lucy Shields was supposed to be here, but she couldn't make it," Mrs Archer said. "She told me she'd vote for you, no matter what, though, so I guess it won't make any difference."

"It's nice to know I've got friends," I said.

And then as we sat down, Mr. Huffines looked at me and said, "Since I'm a Civil War scholar, I was fascinated by your name, because we've got a plaque to General Bragg out front."

"I saw that," I said. "Made me feel right at home."

"I thought it might be a neat thing to have somebody

with the name of a real Confederate general helping our ladies into the church on Sunday morning."

I just smiled at this, and I started to tell 'em that
General Bragg was my great granddaddy, but then I thought
it might just stir up more complications than it was worth,
so I let it drop. Still Mr. Huffines went on, "If we could just
find somebody named Stonewall Jackson to help you, we'd
really have it made," he said. And everybody around the
table began to chuckle at that until I said, "Yeah, that would
be good, wouldn't it? Too bad them guys decided to fight
for the wrong army." And that sort of sobered things up for
a while until Reverend Mann cleared his throat and leaned
over the table and started asking about references, where
else I'd worked and stuff like that, which I told him.

"And are you a Christian?" Mr. Mann said.

"I've always attended the Baptist Church," I said.

"Um hum. And you do believe in Jesus?"

"I never seen any reason not to," I said. And then I
almost busted out laughing because I couldn't help thinking
that if he knew the same Jesus I'd met at the Tiptop Club,
we'd be having a whole different conversation.

"And you wouldn't feel deprived by working here
with us on Sunday morning instead of going to your own
church?"

"Well, seems like we always have to make sacrifices
to better ourselves," I said. And Mr. Mann busted out laughing at that, and then the others started asking their own questions.

It all went along OK. They told me what the job involved and how much it paid and how I would have retirement benefits and health insurance—which really means a lot after you get into your fifties. And I thought I had it sewed up until Mr. Huffines came along with his big question. "I hate to get into this kind of thing," he said, "but we have to ask it, since our sexton works so closely with the property and money and welfare of our parishioners."

"What's that?" I said.

And he said, "Have you ever been arrested and convicted of any crime?"

Oh Lord! I really didn't expect it. Were they really gonna dig up that one conviction from over thirty years ago to sink me with now? At first, I started to say no. Who in the hell was gonna dig up a conviction that's over thirty years old? But then I thought, tell the truth, Braxton. It may keep you from getting this job, but if you lie about it and somebody finds out, you'll really be done for. I guess all this shows I've got a really strong heart, because by then my heart was pumping away just like I'd been cornered again by the man with the butcher knife. I could hear it in my voice when I started talking, pounding away like somebody was slappin' me on the back with every word I spoke. "Well, I tell you, Mr. Huffines," I said, wishing I could get my voice under control, "when I was eighteen and in high school, I was convicted of assault on a guy who stole my overcoat."

"On the guy who stole your overcoat?"

"Yessir. I guess I punished him a little too much."

Mr. Huffines asked about the dates and the court and the penalty and all that, and I knew he was gonna look it up, so I told him all I could. And then, Mrs. Archer suggested we might take a tour of the building and grounds so I would know what I might be gettin' into. And everybody was just as cordial as you please. "We'll let you know something in the next week or so," Mr. Mann said. "We have to interview two other people, but we'll have our decision soon."

"OK," I said. And I thanked them all and went on back to my truck, kickin' myself every which way and thinkin', you stupid fucker. And you did it to yourself. To yourself! It's tough enough travelin' through life in a dark skin, but travelin' under the dark cloud of a conviction— even one that's over thirty years old—don't leave no place to escape. There won't a chance in hell they'd hire me for that job now, I thought. The whole thing just came up on me like somebody had a rope around my throat. There I was dressed up in my good clothes, walkin' into that fancy church where my great granddaddy's name was on the wall and feelin' like I couldn't tell 'em he was my great granddaddy. And those people, so 'amused' at a black guy named after a Confederate general—and then goin' back over thirty years to dig up that one conviction when I was a kid, not lookin' at the fact that I been clean ever since. Made me want to hit somebody. I remember once when I was little, my grandmother tried to drown me. I don't know why she wanted to drown me, but she did. I was just about eight or nine years old and she was keepin' me while my folks were at work, and I was in the bathtub full of water when she came in and pushed me under. Just held me there, pushin' on the top of my head and holdin' me down while I squirmed and flailed until I finally got her hand in my mouth and bit her. Gave her a scar that lasted all her life. But I got out of that bathtub. And that's the way I felt that morning comin' out of that church, like I was bein' held under water and couldn't get my breath. I just had to ride around for a while lettin' the wind blow in my face. Even the thought of maybe seein' Elva or catchin' the man in snakeskin boots or makin' an extra thousand dollars for the weekend's work at the Museum—none of it seemed to matter one way or another, I felt so hemmed in.

But after a while I went on home and changed out of my Sunday suit and into my regular clothes, and the first place I had to go was over to the Archer's house to give them a lick and a promise before I went back to the Museum to get everything ready for the following day.

There was nobody at the Archer's house, so I could work quicker without takin' time to talk, except that I did take some time and used their telephone to call Elva again. This time the phone rang but nobody answered. So I hung up after about ten rings and called my brother Billy who I knew was finished teaching for the day. "Billy," I said, "did you get to talk to her?"

"Yeah," he said. "I told her."

"And what did she say?"

"She said she'd talk to you if you reached her there at the house, but she didn't know whether she should see you or not."

"Why is that?"

"She didn't say, but I'd guess it has something to do with you being married and all."

"I'm married," I said, "but I ain't dead."

"Well, I'm just telling you what she said. If you can't reach her at the house, your only other chance is to catch her at the revival tomorrow night."

"Shit! I got about as much chance doin' that as a nigger has tryin' to join the Ku Klux Klan. But OK. Thanks. I'll do the best I can." So, I hung up and dialed Elva again with the same results, and by then it was time for me to head for the Museum.

The kids were there waitin' for me the way I'd told 'em, along with the other people Lucy Shields had hired, and I realized the minute I walked in that this was going to be a kind of rehearsal day. Everybody had a place and an assignment and a special kind of costume to wear. One woman was workin' with a bunch of guys dressed up like Russian Cossack soldiers who were supposed to help in any way they could, takin' glasses when they were empty, assisting people with coats, pointing the way toward the rest rooms, and herding the crowd toward the dining room when the cocktail hour was over. The German chef and his assistant were screamin' at the Mexican waiters and assigning them their tables and their routes of travel back and forth so they wouldn't run into each other. And Lucy Shields said my job was to assign each of my workers a special sector to be responsible for. So I made sure everybody had the right brooms and mops and portable trash baskets so they could be on the spot and take all the trash out to the big dumpster on the side of the building. And then I made sure they all knew what kind of clothes they were supposed to wear, and the only one to complain was Clarice. "Braxton," she said. "I'm not sure I like this job. I wanted to come here to enjoy the art, not work on somebody's shit detail."

Billy had told me she had a mouth on her, but I said, "Listen, Clarice. Your job is to do your work and earn your money. You can come back next week and enjoy the art." And then I motioned for her to come with me, and I took her over by the center table that was already decorated with a large silver centerpiece filled with red roses that poured over the side toward these little horn shaped things that were filled with artichokes and limes and lilies. "This is the prettiest table in the place," I told Clarice, "and this is where I want you to work tomorrow 'cause you're gonna be the prettiest girl in the place, whether you realize it or not." She kind of looked down embarrassed at that, and then I told her, "Your job is to do your work and not be bothered by all the bullshit that's goin' on." And that seemed to calm her down.

So by the time I left the Museum that afternoon, I figured we'd have everything pretty near ready to go when things started the next night. And I realized it was time for me to get back to thinkin' about the really important things—things like Alphonso Ramirez and the twenty thousand dollars, for example. Time to go hunting, I thought, time to make a plan.

Still, the first thing I did was call Elva again from the pay phone in the lobby, and this time I got her brother. "Yeah," he told me, "she said you might call. But she's already gone to a rehearsal over at the church."

"You mean she's there now?"

"Yeah, workin' with Ollie—the guy that was singin' last night."

"OK," I said. "I'll call later." And then I thought maybe I could just get over there and catch her without anybody else around. So once again, I headed for my truck.

Since so much of the parking lot had been taken up by the big tent, I had parked on the street that day, and just as I came out the side door of the Museum and walked around the corner, I saw Officer Collins, the same policeman who had helped us that day at the clinic when we had so much trouble with that drunk woman and her daughter. He was parked in his squad car up near the corner. I waved at him as I went by, and then I stopped and went back. He rolled down his window and asked how I was and all, and then I said, "I need some advice."

"What about?" he said.

I thought for a minute, and then I said, "About the best way to report it, if you spot a criminal who's wanted by the law."

"I can give you some numbers to call," he said. "Or you can call me. What you got?"

"I seen somebody," I said, and for a minute I stalled

for time, wondering if I should tell him what I knew. "He's a fugitive," I said. And then I thought, what the hell, and I reached in my pocket and pulled out the poster for Alphonso Ramirez. "This guy," I said. "I've seen him. I recognized him by his snakeskin boots."

Officer Collins looked at the poster and just whistled. "You've seen him?"

"A lot," I said.

"Where?"

And it was then I got a little cagey. "All over town... and out in the county. The first time was out at Greentop Sporting Goods when he was buying a pistol. He just keeps showin' up different places."

"Well, I tell you one thing," Collins said. "Don't try to bring him in yourself."

"Oh, no sir, not a chance of that," I said, "But if I see him...if I've got him spotted, what do I do?"

"Call me," Collins said. "Any time, day or night." He pulled out a note pad. And if you can't get me, here are some other people you can call."

"Even if he's in the county?"

"Even if he's in the county—unless you know somebody out there. We'll get in touch with the county police."

"OK," I said. "I'm countin' on you for backup."

"Backup, hell," Collins said. "You count on us to do the whole thing once you've spotted him." He handed me back the poster. "And Braxton, stay out of his way, because this guy will kill you as quick as look at you."

"Tell me about it," I said. I thanked him and went on my way to the truck, a little later than I wanted to be, but thinkin', OK, now, sump'n may be gonna work out after all. Maybe sump'n might work for me and Elva, too. And I jumped in the truck and headed for Emmanuel Baptist Church.

The door to their Sunday school building was open, and I went in beside the church office, and pretty soon I heard piano music and somebody singing, and I followed it through the side door to the sanctuary. There she was, playin' for the same light dude that had been singin' the night before, and just as I came in, she stood up and said, "Well, that'll have to do, for today," and started down the steps from the stage toward me. Oh, my God! She was lookin' mighty pretty and my heart was beatin' clear out of my chest, and then as she came closer, she looked away from the other guy and looked at me. For just a minute, I don't think she recognized me, and then she said, "Braxton, is that you?"

And I said, "Yeah, Honey, it's me."

And she said, "Oh my goodness! Braxton! How are you?" And she came on toward me like she might be goin' to hug me or kiss me or sump'n, but she didn't. She just took both of my hands in hers and said, "You're lookin' mighty well."

And I said, "You are, too."

"Let me introduce you to my partner, Ollie Clay," she said. "Ollie, this is an old friend, Braxton Bragg." And then she said to me, "Ollie is my musical partner."

I shook hands with the dude. Had a handshake like a wet eel. And then I said, "Will there be some time we might get together—you know, just talk a little while?"

And she said, "Well, maybe after the revival tomorrow night. You are going to be at the revival, aren't you?"

"Oh sure," I said, "sure, wouldn't miss it for the world," all the while thinkin', oh shit! there's no way in hell I can be at that revival tomorrow night. "Is there any other time? later today or the day after the revival?" I said.

"I just don't know when it would be," she said. "We're on the way to a dinner now, and I think I'm going' back to Chicago the morning after. But come tomorrow night, and we'll see if we can arrange something." And she shook my hand like I might have been an insurance salesman or something and turned to the other guy, "Come on, Ollie, we'd better run now," and she started toward the door.

"Bye, Elva," I said. "See you tomorrow."

And she looked back and said, "Yeah. See you tomorrow," and walked out through the door. But I could tell by the way she was clutchin' Ollie's arm that there was probably more between them than a musical friendship.

"Yeah," I said. "See you tomorrow."

12

Oh My God! Why is it everything just keeps hanging? Like a rock balanced on the edge of a cliff. Not now but maybe later. You apply for a job and they say, "We'll get back to you." You try to see a woman, and she says, "Come back tomorrow." Why can't anybody just say YES? I remember once when I was a kid, I went deer hunting with my granddaddy's old single shot Iver Johnson shotgun. The ammunition must have been at least twenty-five years old even then, but I went out early one morning and was sittin' there on a log just back from a place where I'd seen the deer walk by, sittin' there just as quiet as you please, you know, when I started hearin' the crinkle of leaves up ahead, and gradually through the trees I could see three deer comin' my way, three deer walkin' slowly—you know how they do—step, by step, by step—and one of 'em was the biggest old buck I'd ever seen. Must have had ten points on his antlers. Damn, talk about your heart beating! Mine was goin' like a riveting machine and I was quiverin' all over, but I got that old Iver Johnson up to my shoulder and waited, and just as that old buck stepped into the clearing, I pulled down on him, and Click! was all I got. Click! I swear to you. I'd done everything right. My aim was right at his heart, I pulled the trigger, the hammer fell, and Click! I thought my chest was gonna explode. I had enough time to cock the hammer and try again, but them deer weren't waitin' around. They heard that second click and jumped out of that clearing like they might have been swingin' from a trapeze wire, and then a moment later, the gun fired: Ka Boom! Damn gun near'bout knocked me down. A hang fire! And sometimes now, it seems I've spent an ungodly amount of my life waitin' for things to go off on time and almost nothin' ever does.

"You must be doin' sump'n wrong, Braxton," I said to myself as I got in my truck, "What are you gonna do to make things better? Are you prepared for whatever might come up?" I went over a kind of checklist in my mind. Everything for the big Museum deal was in place; all my cleaning supplies were in place; I had a flashlight and batteries; I had a good pistol to help me take care of the dark corners. And then, I thought, what're you gonna do if you spot Alphonso Ramirez? And suddenly this little scenario began to form in my mind: I would be waiting in the parking lot and I could see him walkin' from his big Continental into the Mexican restaurant; I would wait for him to get inside and get comfortable. And then I'd call Officer Collins. From where? I thought. Where you gonna call from? And suppose Old Snakeskin don't stay at the restaurant. Suppose he gets back in his car and drives off. What you gonna do then? "Hell, Braxton," I said out loud, "you better get your ass in gear. This is big time stuff you're dealin' with." And I realized for the first time that I needed a cell phone. Right now. Today. Or else this whole Ramirez deal could be just another big CLICK! and somebody else was liable to walk off with the $20,000. And on that afternoon, as soon as I could find a place, I went into a phone store and got myself lined up for service. I'd never even wanted a cell phone before because I thought people looked so damn silly walkin' around or driving with a phone in their face. But now I saw how it could be really helpful—a little bitty phone I could carry in my pocket. Now I was ready, I thought. All I'd have to do was dial Officer Collins's number, and the big bucks would be comin' in. After I'd found Old Snakeskin, of course, after I'd got him in a corner. And I started trying to picture it in my mind again as I headed on toward the Corporation Headquarters. Where would it be? I wondered. At the restaurant? In a filling station? On the side of the road?

I pulled into the alley behind the Corporation just after closin' time, and no sooner did I get out of the truck than I ran smack into Mr. Shields and Miss Blowzer comin' out the back door.

I swear to you, Archibald Shields is some dude, always got a smile on his face as though nothing has ever gone wrong in his whole damn life, sort of reminds me of that guy Kenneth Lay at Enron Corporation. There he was walkin' out the door with Miss Blowzer on his arm and waving at me and callin' hello as if he didn't know good and well that I'd walked in on the two of 'em while they were fuckin' their brains out in his office. I guess he figures that if you act like sump'n ain't a problem, it ain't a problem. Anyway, he called out and said, "So glad you're able to help out at the

Museum, Braxton. It means a lot to Lucy to know you've got those cleanup jobs under control over there."

"Yessir," I said. "Glad I can help out."

And then, big as brass, he says, "You remember Miss Blowzer, don't you?"

"Oh yes," I said. "I remember Miss Blowzer quite well." And all of a sudden, she was blushin' red as a Coca-Cola sign. I guess that's one thing that black folks have over white folks—you can't see our embarrassments so easy.

Anyway, I finished up at the Corporation early, and then there were two other places I wanted to go before I headed back to the Museum for the last run-through before the big event—the clinic and the karate studio.

The main thing I wanted to do at the clinic was pick up my paycheck or else get Alice to mail it to the bank for me if it wasn't ready, but when I got there, the place was in an uproar. The police were there, the insurance people were there. God knows who all. "Braxton," Alice said, "we've lost a shipment of drugs."

"A shipment of drugs?"

"Yeah. The man delivered it late yesterday, and it's gone today."

"Did somebody break in?"

"Not so we can tell. You got any ideas?"

"Naw," I said. "I don't know nothin' about it." But then, of course, it was no more'n a second before I remembered the box of drugs I'd found on the back steps. I started to say something, but then I thought better of it because the police detective came over about that time and I thought there won't no advantage of tellin' anybody I'd found a box of drugs and thrown 'em away.

"Who is this?" the detective said to Alice when he saw me, and she told him. "I'm Detective Short," he said to me, and he pulled back the collar of this little blue windbreaker he was wearin' over his tee shirt to show me his badge. "Were you here last night?" he asked me, and just as he asked me that, Frances and Dr. Redfield came out the back room and were just standing there lookin' at me.

"Yessir," I said. "Worked till about two o'clock this morning."

"You always work that late?"

"I do most of my work at night, yessir."

"Braxton, that box of drugs was right there on the table by the door," Frances said, "right where I set it when I signed for it."

There was somethin' about her tone that made me feel all of a sudden like they all somehow thought I had somethin' to do with the lost drugs, and my routine stop by the clinic was fast changing into something else.

"There was no box on the table when I got here last night," I said. "But I'll tell you what I did see. I found a box of hypodermic needles layin' out there on the back steps."

"Hypodermic needles! What were hypodermic needles doing on the back steps?" Detective Short said.

"I don't know what they were doin' there. But I threw 'em in a trash bag and hauled 'em away to the dump,"

I told him.

"But no drugs?"

"I don't know nothin' about no drugs." It was gettin' to be a tight moment, I tell you. I knew that if I told 'em I'd found the drugs outside and throwed 'em in the trash along with the needles, they were all gonna say they didn't believe me. Certainly Detective Short wouldn't believe me, and that could lead to all sorts of problems. They started talkin' about the other employees—like Elwood, the gay orderly, and Maybel, the fat practical nurse who worked earlier in the day. So I said, "If you all don't need me anymore, I'd like to pick up my check and get on to my next job," and Dr. Redfield motioned for me to come into his office.

"Don't worry about this stuff, Braxton," he said. "I know you're not involved. But we had to call the police for the sake of the insurance, if nothing else."

"OK," I said. "I appreciate you saying that."

And then he looked sort of apologetic. "But we haven't got the checks yet," he said, "because the accountant hasn't sent them over. Can you stop by early tomorrow?"

"It'll be hard," I said. "I've got a big job earlier to-morrow. But I'll try."

"I'm sorry," he said. "But I promise to have it tomor-row."

I thanked him then, and although I felt frustrated as hell about the check, I breathed easier as I went out of there thinkin' how easy it is for one little thing to screw up your whole damn day, maybe even screw up your whole damn life, if it lands wrong. Still, I told myself, "Stay cool, Braxton. You got some important things to do." And I jumped in my truck and headed for my afternoon "surveillance" run to the karate studio and the Mexican restaurant.

It was too early for the crazies and the serious criminals to be out and I knew it, but still you can't afford to get too set in your expectations. One of the reasons a guy like Alphonso Ramirez was still walking around was that he never got too set in his ways and nobody could ever guess what he was gonna do next.

Anyway, on this day everything around the restaurant seemed quiet, so I parked in the edge of the parking lot next to the shrubs and just watched things for a while till I started getting hungry from the smell of food that was blowin' out of the kitchen. Now I hadn't even thought about goin' inside the place before. I mean, hell, I grew up during segregation years when a nigger didn't even think of goin' into a white man's restaurant unless he was lookin' for trouble. And God only knew what you might find if you went into a brown man's restaurant. But on that day, I felt just pissed off enough to try anything, and I reached under the seat of the pickup for my little semi-automatic Walthur, stuck it in my pocket and headed toward the door. I wasn't planning to shoot the place up, you understand, but if anybody got me in a corner, I wasn't gonna let 'em do nothin' without payin' for it.

In any case, the first thing that hit me inside the place was the noise. Music was blarin' over the loud speaker—

you know, lots of trumpets and drums and somebody singin'
so loud in Spanish, I thought it was gonna deafen me. Took
me a minute to get my bearings, and then when my eyes adjusted to the light, they had to get used to the fact that some
part of every wall was painted red. Made your eyes pop, all
that red jumpin' out at you. But I found a table in one corner
so I could see the whole room, and I realized in a minute,
after lookin' around me at the brown Mexicans in the place,
that it was gonna be really hard for a black guy to sit there
for very long and not be noticed. So when this little waiter
came over, I ordered a burrito and a glass of beer and ate as
fast as I could so I could get out of there. It didn't take me
long, but even so, when I was standing at the counter to pay
for my food, I looked up and here came the same two guys
who had been with Ramirez on the night I found the dead
man in the restroom at the service station, and I knew that
the big man himself must be somewhere close behind.

 I tell you, that sort of thing does something to you.
The guy behind the cash register made change for the twenty
I gave him, and I dropped it all over the floor when he handed it to me. Had quarters and nickels rollin' every which
way. Even one of Ramirez's boys kicked a quarter back in
my direction when it rolled up against his shoe. "Thanks,"
I said, and then I slipped on outside hopin' he didn't pay me
no mind.

 "You've got to get hold of yourself, Braxton," I said
to myself as I walked across the lot. "You can't afford to get
all nervous when you come face to face with the big man."

And I sat in the pickup for a while and started imagining the scene, how I'd react if Ramirez himself would walk in, how I'd be just as cool as you please, just the way I was when Tami walked across the room naked in Mr. Seidell's apartment. Tami, of course, was not strapped with a 9-millimeter pistol, and that did make a difference. But still, I knew I had to do it. "If you want big bucks, you've got to put your ass on the line to get it," I said to myself. "So get ready. Nerves of steel." And I sat there in the truck and started picturing one scene after another and how I'd deal with it if it happened, figuring what my choices would be.

I waited as long as I could that night to see if Ramirez's big Continental would pull up before I had to leave, but on that evening Ramirez never showed. So I went on to my next job thinkin' about that business of waiting, how everything requires waiting: Elva, the church job, the pay check, Alphonso Ramirez...not today but try tomorrow. OK, I thought. OK. It ain't gonna happen today...but sooner or later. I'm ready. I'm more than ready. Sooner or later this nigger's gonna make his mark, one way or another.

I wasn't finished at the clinic, of course. I still had to go back that night after closing hours and see the place was cleaned up and ready for business the next morning. So as soon as I finished checkin' everything out at the Museum, I headed back. The clinic wasn't the most perfect job in the world, of course, and it worried me a lot, but still, the people were nice and the pay was pretty good, when they remembered to get it to me, so I wanted to do right by 'em.

Everything was quiet that night, with nothin' and nobody to get in my way up until about midnight when I decided to check the front porch. Now the door to the porch usually stays closed and bolted and that porch never gets used, but there in the early fall, the leaves had already started falling and blowing onto the floor, so I decided to sweep 'em off. There were a couple of heavy iron chairs out there—for looks mostly. And when I got through sweeping, I decided to sit in one and smoke a cigarette. It was the first time I'd really sat down to relax for the whole day. But no sooner had I lit up than I heard this woman's voice callin' to me from the street, "Hi there!" she said. She was standing at the end of the walkway, and she must have seen the light when I flicked my zippo. "Haven't seen you in a long time," she said.

It was dark, of course, but in the streetlight I could see it was a blonde white woman who I'd never seen before in my life. But still, I didn't want to be impolite, so I said, "Good evening." Just that and nothin' more. But by this time, she was halfway up the walk.

"I thought you had given up this job," she said.

"Naw, I ain't give it up," I told her. "We just have a little tighter security than we used to have." By now, she was comin' up the steps, so I stood and closed the door behind me. Man or woman, you can't tell what nobody out on North Boulevard is gonna do after midnight.

"You think I'm going to try to break in?" she said.

"No," I told her. "But that door is supposed to stay closed."

"You must think I'm crazy, if you think I'd try to get past you," she said. "Big strong man like you...I wouldn't have a chance." By now she was standing right in front of me, and I could see she won't a bad lookin' woman. Looked pretty good, in fact, about thirty-five and looked a good many notches up from the usual woman you're liable to find roamin' the Boulevard after midnight. "But you could at least offer me a cigarette," she said. "I've cut down, but I do need a cigarette before I go to bed at night."

"Well, OK," I said. I didn't want her to stick around, but I couldn't see any special harm in givin' her a cigarette, so I shook one out of the pack and lit it for her, and she inhaled that first big puff in kind of a gasp, like she'd been hungerin' for it all day.

"That's great," she said, "really great." And then she looked up at me and said, "I've seen you workin' over here lots of times. Don't you get lonesome workin' in there all by yourself so late at night?"

It was then I realized I had to size things up mighty fast. What was she after? I wondered. Was she after drugs or was she workin' for the pro-lifers or did she just want a little somethin' on the side? She was standing there close to me and exhaling smoke like a volcano, but still, by the time she was that close, I could smell the perfume she was wearin'—which mixed with the cigarette smoke real good, you understand. Nice smell. But still, there were all sorts of alarm bells goin' off in my head. What the hell did this good lookin' white woman want with me on the porch of the clinic

at 1:00 AM? "Don't you, hunh?" she said, "get lonesome?"
And she reached up and touched my cheek.

"No," I said. "I got plenty to keep me busy inside. I
don't get lonesome."

"Aw, I don't believe that," she said, "not a strong
man like you." And by this time she was pressin' herself up
against me.

Now I'd be lyin' if I didn't admit that for a minute I
was a little bit tempted. First, she was a good lookin' woman,
and then there's this thing that goes on sometimes between
white women and black men that nobody ever talks about.
I think the women get curious, you know, a kind of 'what's
it like to make it with a black guy?' sort of thing. And the
black guys, well, you know, are more than willing to satisfy
their curiosity. But this was somethin' different. I was at
the clinic, and this woman had just walked up off the street.
"How come you've seen me workin' over here so much?" I
said.

"Oh, I've got an eye for a good lookin' man, Braxton," she said.

"How did you know my name?"

"I've been checkin' up on you. I've been lookin' at
you for a long time."

"Really?"

"Yeah."

"You live around here?"

"Right over there," she said, "in the middle of the
block." And she pointed to a house right next door to the

Catholic Church, which made my alarm bells go off even more.

"What's your name?" I said.

"Angelica," she said. "And I bet, if you'd invite me inside, I'd let you know just how angelic I can be."

"Um hum," I said. And then I began to get the whole picture. "I tell you what, Angelica," I told her. "Let me go inside for just a minute and see what I can arrange to make us comfortable."

"I'll come with you," she said.

"No, no. I think I better go look first," I told her. But by this time, she was throwin' her arms around me and grabbin' my free hand and tryin' to press it against her tits.

"You want to keep me with you, Braxton," she said. "You want to keep me with you."

"I'll come back and get you," I said. And I started pullin' away toward the door.

"If you leave me, you're making a big mistake," she said.

I turned, tryin' to unlock the door with my key in order to get back inside, but she wouldn't let me go. "Look," I said. "I've got to go in there, and I'd appreciate it if you'd turn me loose."

"No, Braxton, no," she said. "I've waited a long time for this and I don't want to let you out of my sight."

By this time I had the key in the lock, but as I turned it, she threw her shoulder against the door and tried to push inside. I grabbed her, of course, and things were gettin' kind of loud by then. "No," I said. "No, I am not lettin' you in there!" And I pulled her back and slipped in front of her, but still she was pushin', tryin' to get past me, so I pushed her back, maybe a little harder than I meant to, and she tripped and fell backwards right on her butt.

"You son of a bitch!" she shouted, "You perfect son of a bitch!" And she went on callin' me a few other choice things, yelling at the top of her voice as I slipped inside and slammed the door.

Now, I was sorry I pushed her down. I really didn't mean to do that. But it did give me a chance to get away, and I threw the bolt as tight as I could. Of course, she won't givin' up. She commenced to pound on the door and scream like somebody was tryin' to kill her, and I knew there won't but one thing for me to do. So I grabbed the nearest tele-phone and dialed the police emergency 911 line, and before I'd even finished giving the dispatcher all my information, three police cars pulled up in the yard of the clinic.

Two policemen came up on the porch with flash-lights and stopped Angelica, and as soon as I saw they had her under control, I went out to talk to 'em. "This man at-tacked me!" she was saying to the policemen. "He attacked me and pushed me down!"

"How about it?" the policeman said to me, "what happened?"

And I told him the whole scene. "She was trying to get inside the clinic and I wouldn't let her," I said.

"Why were you doing it?" they asked Angelica.

"Because this man is an animal!" she screamed, "an animal! He tried to rape me!"

"And you wanted to get inside because he tried to rape you?"

"He's a baby killer!" she shouted. "He works in this clinic from hell and helps people kill babies!"

And of course then, everything became absolutely clear. She was workin' for the pro-lifers, trying to worm her way inside the clinic to do whatever devilment she could. And before anybody could say anything else, I said, "Officer, I want to charge this woman with assault and attempted forcible entry into the clinic." Oh, I was ready, you see. I'd been reading the papers and listening to "America's Most Wanted" on TV, so I knew the legal terms and phrases pretty good.

"Will you come to court to testify?" the policeman said.

"Oh yes sir, I sure will," I told him. "I'll go with you right now to swear out the warrant." And that's where I spent the rest of the night, at police headquarters and the lockup.

Turned out the woman was a nun. And it won't no more than fifteen minutes after she'd made her allotted phone call that police headquarters was near'bout filled with priests and nuns and all sorts of people there to support Sister Angelica. The magistrate, of course, after receiving Angelica's promise to appear in court on the trial date, released her on her own recognizance, and she went off with her buddies from the church.

"You never can tell what's gonna happen next, can you?" I said to the policeman that brought her in.

And he said, "No, you sure can't. At least, not in this case, you can't. But then, maybe you never can tell."

13

When I woke up on Friday morning the sky was so red I thought there was a fire in eastern Henrico County. And of course, as soon as I opened my eyes more and saw it was coming from the clouds and not from the ground, I remembered my granddaddy's little rhyme: "Red sky at morning, sailor take warning." Funny the things you think about right after you wake up. My granddaddy would study the clouds and nod. "Gonna be a bad storm today," he'd say. "Mark what I tell you." And he was right most of the time.

"Better take your umbrella," I told Sadie as she went out the door, but she just smiled and waved at me and went on out leaving me thinking what a day this one was gonna be.

Since I'd never got to the karate studio the night before, I had to catch them before they opened in the morning. So I ate some breakfast in a hurry and headed on out there. By then, of course, the sky had stopped being red and had turned into an angry dark gray, and the wind was blowin' really strong—you know, sudden heavy gusts pushing out of the east. And I got to thinkin' about the tent behind the Museum and all the work we'd done to make the place look pretty. Really be bad if the storm ruined that thing and we had it all to do over again, I thought. I wasn't even sure we could do it over again—not the same way anyhow and certainly not by that night. But when I finished at the karate studio in early afternoon, the rain was comin' down somethin' awful, with lightning and thunder crashing right over the heart of the city like it was under an artillery attack. So I headed on by to look at what was happening to the tent.

By the time I got to Grove Avenue, traffic was in a snarl because all the stoplights were out, and I could tell from lookin' at the houses that nobody had any electricity. I parked as close to the door of the Museum as I could get, but still I was soaked by the time I got inside where people were running around with flashlights and candles and tryin' to work in the near'bout dark, and the first person I recognized was Lucy Shields. "Oh Braxton! This is just awful!" she said. "What're we going to do if we can't get the power back?"

"I don't know," I told her, "but how's the tent?"

She hadn't even been to see the tent yet, but she went out through the archway with me, and the minute we walked under the canvas, we had the answer: the brightest light in the place was comin' through a hole that a flying tree limb had made on the west side. "Oh Jesus!" I said.

And she just stood there like she was paralyzed lookin' at the water comin' in. "What're we going to do?" she said again, "What're we going to do? Is God sending us a message?"

"God may be sending us a message," I told her, "but I don't think the whole story's been told yet. Get that building staff out here and tell 'em to bring a ladder."

I went back in the main building with her, and in the next few minutes we had rounded up the regular staff and found the tallest ladder in the place. "Come on ," I told 'em. "We've got to patch up the hole and dry up the water."

"How you gonna do that?"

"Duct tape," I said. "Get me some canvas and some duct tape—all of which the building and grounds director found, but still, everybody was standing around like nobody wanted to even get near that ladder. "Shit!" I said. "Somebody hold this thing." And I took the cloth and the tape and started up the ladder myself. I don't know where I got the energy to do all this. I guess it was the thought of all my work being spoiled that fired me. But suddenly, I was doin' it like I was supposed to be doin' it.

"Braxton, be careful!" Lucy said.

"I'm bein' careful," I told her. "Just make sure them people hold this ladder." And the upshot of it all was that I did it. I mean, duct tape is wonderful stuff. I'd hate to live in a world without duct tape. But I managed to patch that hole so it could deflect the water and people could begin mopping up the inside. Of course, it was a big help that by the time I got through, the rain had near'bout quit and the wind was beginning to let up. But the patch seemed to hold, and Lucy was dancin' around all excited. "Oh, Braxton, you have saved us," she said, "You have saved us!"

"Well, we'll see," I said. "We'll see. But right now, I'm goin' home and put on some dry clothes."

I called my brother Billy and told him to get his boys and Clarice on over to the Museum as soon as possible to help with the cleanup—the first call I ever made on my new cell phone—and then I headed out.

Now, of course, I was wet and cold in the breeze that was still blowin' pretty strong, but I thought that since I was only a short way from the clinic, maybe I could go by there and pick up my check and put it in the bank on my way home. So a few minutes later, I pulled up in the yard behind the clinic and went in. They didn't have any electricity, either, except in the operating room where they had alternative power, and the waiting room was dark as a cave. Alice had set up a couple of oil lamps in there that gave some light, but still it took a minute for my eyes to adjust, and then when they did, the first people I saw sittin' huddled near the door were Betsy Shields and her friend Dennis. Now, I've got to hand it to Dennis. He was stickin' by that girl. I've seen guys come by and leave their girlfriends off at the curb and then drive away or park somewhere and wait outside in the car while the girl had whatever she was gonna have done, guys that acted like they didn't want to have no part of it. But Dennis, he was right there with his arm around Betsy doin' his best to make her feel OK, and Betsy—well, she was clearly scared to death, and of course, my showing up didn't help her none. "Oh my God, Braxton!" she said when she saw me, "What're you doing here?"

"I work here," I told her.

"Oh, what you must think of me!"

"Don't make no difference what I think," I said, "or what anybody else thinks either. You just go on about your business like you didn't know I was here."

"We can't go on," she said. "The lights are out." And she started crying something awful.

"They won't start another operation till the power's back on," Dennis said. "We're just going to wait a while and see."

"Braxton, you won't tell Mama, will you?" Betsy said. "Don't tell Mama you saw me here."

"I ain't gonna tell your mama nothin'," I said. And then I sort of joked with her, "I don't think I've seen you since you got your new party dress." And she sort of laughed through her tears at that. "Now you just sit there and behave yourself and see what happens next," I said. And I went on down the hall to see if my check was ready.

But it all did sort of get to me. I had watched this girl grow up from a scrawny little ten year old to a sexy seventeen year old, and I'd watched her doing things that her folks didn't seem to notice, and now here she was waitin' in the dark for an abortion while her mama prepared a big, fancy party up the Boulevard. Something seemed out of whack about it. And I realized that I knew more about Lucy Shields's family than Lucy herself knew, in spite of all her family charts. I felt sort of like a banker in a back street bank who knows about accounts that the account holders themselves don't know about...Lucy, for instance, just as innocent as you please, makin' all this hoopla over the Faberge

Easter Eggs while her husband Archibald was bangin' Miss Blowzer at the office and her daughter Betsy was shackin' up with Dennis and getting an abortion at the clinic...and I was the only one who knew about any of it. Oh well, I thought. Nothin' much I could do about none of it, but I did have another job I needed to go to. So I got my check from Dr. Redman's office and headed for the door just as the electricity came back on. "Great," I said, "great. Maybe now things will get back to normal." And I turned to Betsy in the waiting room. "You be strong now," I said. "Be strong." And I patted Dennis on the shoulder as I went toward my truck.

Now, I tell you, that party at the Museum was the damnedest thing I ever saw in my life. I mean, you talk about fancy! I've told about some of it already—the imitation forest around the Volga River and the Hall of Mirrors and the red Revolutionary Room. In fact, the major color of the whole thing was red, both inside the building and out in the tent—red, along with gold and brown—and of course, that was mixed with great big pots of roses and flowers of all kinds. People would walk in and stop and their mouths would drop open, and then they'd say something like, "Oh, my God!" or "Marvelous!" "Spectacular!" "Exquisite!" except for the occasional down to earth woman who'd say something like, "A little gaudy, don't you think?" And then, there was one guy—I heard him but I didn't see him—who walked in behind me and just said, "Holy shit! Which way is the bar?"

But nobody had any complaints about the food: Volga River sturgeon and pheasant served on gold rimmed plates along with ginger pear mousse and "herbed force meat"—whatever that was—while two orchestras were playing the whole time, one inside the building and one out in the tent (which they decided to call "The Crystal Tent") so people could dance. The TV cameras were there and TV people were interviewing the Governor while at least two ex-Governors were out on the dance floor with their wives. Then of course, once they got through talkin' to the people in state government, they had to interview my old buddy Cliff Eastman, the mayor of Richmond, if you remember, along with a few members of City Council. They were about the only black people I saw there—among the invited guests, I mean. I guess there weren't too many black folks in Tsarist Russia in the old days, anyway. But this handful of our elected representatives was right there at this imperial party lookin' like ambassadors from a foreign country among the corporation presidents like Mr. Shields and Mr. Gottwald and Mr. Forbes and people from DuPont and Allied Chemical, all people who I could recognize from pictures I'd seen in the paper. And then there were some artists in the crowd wearing all sorts of weird outfits, and there was at least one movie star—I think it was Anthony Quinn because he was so interested in art—and, well, you name it.

Of course, most of the time, I was running around keeping my eye on the trash and making sure my helpers stayed on top of things, but I saw a lot about the way rich

folks like to celebrate—all those evening gowns and tux-
edos and more jewelry—my Lord!—necklaces, bracelets,
brooches, rings, diamonds, rubies, emeralds. I doubt the
Tsar of Russia himself had much more in his treasury than
what was hanging on the women at that party. I just hoped
they had plenty of cops stationed around the place to guard
'em.

But in spite of the crowds and all the fuss, the party
really ran along pretty smooth for the first couple of hours.
My kids were doin' a good job and the extra trash was next
to nothin', so I began to think about Elva over at the revival
meeting, thinkin' about how pretty she looked and how good
she sounded when she played the piano, and how nice it'd be
if she'd agree to see me after all this was over, and I thought
maybe...just maybe I could slip out for a while and nobody
would notice. I called Ronnie over and told him I was
gonna run an errand but I'd be back in a few minutes, and he
seemed all right about it. So I looked around one more time
just to make sure everything was in place, and then I took off
for the church. Took off, I say, because that's what I did: I
flew, squealin' my tires around corners, drivin' about twenty
or thirty miles over every speed limit in town, barely skim-
min' the road, you know, just hopin' the cops wouldn't stop
me and that Elva wouldn't leave before I got there.

But when I reached the church, I realized there won't
a chance in hell she could've left already because they were
just gettin' started good. They had spotlights shinin' on the
steeple of the church, and I could hear the congregation sing-

ing all the way from the lot where I parked my truck. I'd forgotten how an old-fashioned revival meeting could last near'bout forever. But of course, I couldn't stay forever, and I had to do sump'n quick. So I went inside and walked down the hall to the door behind the sanctuary where I could see Elva and Ollie and the drummer and the choir on the stage beatin' out this song that just about had the congregation dancin' in the aisles. Man, they were goin' at it, clappin' their hands and stompin' their feet hard enough to shake the bricks out of the wall. I don't know what all that stuff had to do with religion, but everybody seemed to be having a good time, and I guess that counts for something. But I wanted 'em to knock it off so I could see Elva and make some plans.

So I just paced up and down in front of the open door until finally the song came to an end and the people started clappin'. The preacher stood up to say a few words and lead the congregation in prayer, and I realized that this would be the time—now or never. And I moved closer where I could stand just inside the stage door and wave to Elva, trying to catch her eye, which I couldn't do for the longest sort of time because she was busy prayin', and then when she finally did look up, she looked sort of irritated when she saw me. I tried not to let it bother me, though. I just motioned to her and smiled as broad as I could and mouthed the words for her to come out and speak to me, but for a minute she didn't seem to understand what I wanted. Then I saw her reach down to the music stand in front of her for a pencil and paper and start scribblin' away in a great fury until she handed the paper to one of the choir members and pointed at me. I didn't know what to expect, of course, but I took the note from the girl and backed out in the hall where the light was better so I could read it. And oh my God! It took me a minute to figure out Elva's handwriting, but then there was no mistake. "Braxton," the note said, "I can't see you tonight or tomorrow or any other time, so don't bug me about it. We had a good time years ago, but that's over. I'm with Ollie now, and there's no point. So goodbye and good luck. Elva."

For a minute, I just stood there lookin' at the note like I might be expecting it to change into something else right there in front of me. But it didn't. I don't know what I had been expecting—if anything—or what had made me even think anything could come out of all this. I hadn't really thought it through. Suppose she had said yes and we'd got somethin' on—would I have left Sadie and gone to Chicago with Elva, or would Elva have left Chicago and come back to Richmond with me? Hell no. I couldn't see any of that happening in a million years. But Elva was something, you know, something that you hold up, no matter what happens, and say, "What if...?" like holding up the cards in a big poker game or the thought of winning the lottery or inheriting a pile of money...or even of putting the finger on Ramirez. What if...? Was that all Ramirez was ever gonna be for me, I wondered, just a $20,000 game of what if? But Elva...damn.... What if I had ended up with this woman I'd always dreamed of bein' with? How would that have changed my life? But now I knew I'd never find out. I knew it won't ever gonna happen.

I read the note again. "...Goodbye and good luck. Elva." And I just said, "Shit!" Spoke it out good and loud right there in the hall so it echoed off the wall. "Shit and God damn!" The congregation probably heard me all the way to the back of the church, "Shit and God damn!" while they were still sayin' their prayers, and I just walked on out to my truck through a kind of foggy mist that was beginnin' to rise off the ground.

"OK," I said. "OK. That's that. One down. OK." But I didn't drive so fast as I went on back downtown. "God damn!"

14

My work started up again the instant I walked back inside the Museum. Most people had finished dinner, but the bars were workin' overtime, and the dance floors were full. The band was blarin' away with the 'Macarena,' the dance that was so popular that year, and the people who weren't dancin' were roaming through the galleries 'oohing' and 'ahhing' over all those jewel-encrusted Faberge designs, and I walked into the building just in time to see a man trip and come tumbling down those marble steps at the front. He looked like he might have been in his seventies, a white haired guy with a glass in one hand and his eyes on some woman who was passin' by. His feet shot up in the air, and he rolled one way while his glass flew off another. Sounded like a bomb going off when his glass hit that marble floor. But of course, I tried to get to him fast as I could. I eased him down the last two steps and laid him flat on the floor as two guards came to help me while I reached in my pocket for my cell phone to call an ambulance— the second time I'd used my phone. The man looked really bad by then because he'd hit his head, but the ambulance crew didn't take no time to get there, so I figured he'd be OK and I'd better go clean up the broken glass before somebody else tripped on the stairs. But I could see that as things got livelier, just about anything could happen, so I called my crew and told 'em to keep a special eye out. And it won't more than ten minutes later, while I was busy sweeping up some spilled food by the dance floor, I looked down and saw a piece of jewelry in my dust pan. I mean a big piece of jewelry. Gold—all covered with stones so flashy they near'bout put your eyes out. A brooch. I pulled it out of the mess and cleaned it off, and just for a minute I thought, wow, that thing must be worth a fortune and nobody knows I've got it. But I took it on to the guard's office and turned it over to Lost and Found. I later heard the thing was worth about $10,000, according to the guy that picked it up at the end of the night. But it just goes to show what kind of money we're talkin' about at that party.

Well, things bubbled along for another hour or two, and then all of a sudden it was over. People were still out on the floor dancing away close to midnight when the bandleader said a few words into the microphone, and the band just switched over to "Good Night Ladies," and that was it. The music stopped. Complete silence for a few seconds. Like the electricity had been turned off again. And it was kind of spooky, after all the noise and the clinking glasses and the laughter when people were just left with nothing more than the sound of their own voices as they picked up their coats.

But they left pretty quick after the music quit playin', and that's when we really went to work. We cleared that place up in next to no time. Before one o'clock, the dishes were cleared, the glasses collected, the flowers given away or thrown out, and I was back on the street with my own thoughts, walkin' to my truck so I could be on the way to my next job. I felt like I'd just been to something really important, but now it was over and I wasn't exactly sure what it had been. I had made some money, yeah, and the Museum had made some money. The paper later said they'd taken in close to two million dollars on that shindig. But I knew now that Elva was gone forever, and I knew I probably wasn't going to get the sexton's job at the Episcopal church, and here I was going back to the clinic just like always—only a little later than usual—and nothin' had changed. At least that's what I thought at one o'clock in the morning.

Now most people don't know that there are a lot of wild animals in Richmond. You won't know about most of 'em unless you're out a lot late at night, like I am. I've seen full-grown deer just down from the Museum at two o'clock in the morning. And from Byrd Park on west along Cary Street Road, well that's like home territory to 'em. They wander up from the river, and since there's nobody to shoot 'em, they just bed down and come out at night to chew on people's azaleas when there's nobody around.

But beside the deer, there are foxes and owls and hawks and water moccasins and raccoons and possums, all hiding in the parks and in vacant lots and generally keeping out of sight until you walk up on 'em in the dark. Raccoons and possums are the worst because they know how to get the lids off garbage cans and how to spread out the trash till they find exactly what they're lookin' for.

Well, that night it was possums. When I drove up to the back of the clinic just after one o'clock, I thought the street people had been at it again. There was trash spread outside the dumpster, and then I saw right away that the clinic people had started leaving them red bio-hazard bags outside again. The whole thing just made me tired.

"Nobody ever learns nothin'," I said to myself. And then, while I was still sittin' there in the truck with the lights on, I saw him—a big fat possum, maybe the biggest possum I ever saw in my life, comin' out from behind one of them bio-hazard bags, and his face was blood red. It took me a minute to understand it all, but when I did, it hit me like a slap in the face. That possum had had his head stuck through a hole in one of them bags. Oh my God! It near'bout paralyzed me there for a minute while it all sank in: his face was covered with human blood and he'd been eating human body parts! Human remains! I just couldn't move when I realized what was goin' on, and that feeling of nausea washed over me almost as bad as it was the night I had stepped on the bag of fetuses. I didn't throw up this time, but I felt weak. Human body parts! I just couldn't handle it. And I think something broke inside me that night. Human body parts. I couldn't help but wonder if Betsy Shields's fetus—the one she'd got rid of that afternoon—had been among the fetuses this possum had just eaten. Oh my God! There was something about it all that made me feel so sad, maybe the saddest I ever felt in my life. Sad about everything in the world. I remember there was a song my Aunt Mary used to sing when she was workin', back in the days when I was young, helpin' her in her house cleaning jobs. She'd be dusting furniture or polishing a table and singin' soft like to herself, "Sometimes I feel like a motherless child." Well, that night I realized what that song was really all about—"Sometimes I feel like a motherless child a long way from home." Really sad.

But of course, I couldn't just sit there for the rest of the night staring at a bloody possum, so I got out the truck and scared the bastard off. And then I thought to myself, I just can't do it no more. I just can't do it. I'll haul this trash away and I'll get the trash from inside. But I just can't clean the building tonight. I just can't. And then I remembered the Tiptop Club. Great God A'mighty! With all the stuff goin' on through the day, I'd forgot about it, and now the thought of it came back like a kind of black and red thundercloud. I didn't want to clean the clinic, and I didn't want to clean the Tiptop Club. I wanted to go home and go to sleep. But I'd promised Mr. Seidell. "Braxton, you must be the craziest nigger God ever made," I said to myself. "Somewhere along the way, you've got to learn to say no to people." But I'd promised. So I collected the trash and went in and cleaned the operating room and the recovery room while I was at it. And then I washed up real good, throwing lots of cold water on my face, and headed back to my truck. A promise was a promise, after all, and at least on that night, I'd make good on it. So off I went.

There was next to nobody on the road, so once I got

across the river, I was at the Tiptop Club pretty quick, just before closing time. I found Boris, and he unlocked the back door for me so I could take my stuff inside. And then he led me on down this hall between the dressing rooms as we went toward the stage. I tell you, that hallway was just full of girls wearin' next to nothin', some wearing little g-strings or bikini panties and these push-up bras that made 'em look like they were about to spill out over the top, and some with see-through tops, and some with just their g-strings and nothin' else. Every now and then, Boris had to reach out and pat one of 'em on the ass, but they all seemed good natured about it, gigglin' and flirtin' with him, while I, of course, kept my hands to myself—which I have always done, unless a woman made it really clear she wanted to be touched. They were all just as nice as you please toward me, you understand, speaking to me as I came along the hall and not in the least timid about being naked, but I barely knew these girls, and I didn't want no trouble, so I just spoke to 'em and followed Boris on up to the doorway that opened toward the stage.

Teresa was still the headliner for that week's show, and her music was already throbbing and thumping away as I walked along, and I could hear Jesus's voice over the public address system as he introduced her: "And now, Ladies and Gentlemen, put your hands together and greet the lovely TERESA" as she came out for her closing act. I just stood there beside the door watchin' while she began to spin and shake and wiggle, grinding her hips from side to side as she shimmied out of her suit and moved from customer to customer. She was down to her g-string in a couple of minutes, and then she bent over and rolled her ass right in the faces of the guys who were sitting at stage side. It was different from the first time I saw her, and man! It was somethin' awful! After a couple of minutes watchin' this sort of thing, I plumb forgot about Elva and Betsy and bloody possums and near'bout everything else in my life. It does us no special credit, I guess, but I tell you, the sight of a naked woman in motion can clear out a man's mind quicker than anything I know.

Of course, by this time, Teresa was collecting quite a fortune in bills stuck under her garter and into the band of her g-string, and the more she wiggled and the closer she got into the faces of the guys, the bigger the tips they stuck under her elastic. It started with ones, but after a minute I could see fives and tens and twenties. The guys were wavin' their bills and yellin' and eggin' her on and motioning for her to come closer, and this was before she had even taken off the tiny little brassiere she was wearing. First she'd wiggle her tail, and then she'd go to each one and get down on her knees and let 'em look down right in between her titties, and then she'd be back on her feet twisting and turning to one side and then the other as she reached back feelin' for the hook on her brassiere, teasing us, you understand, until after a great long turn, she unhooked it and hurled it out over the audience as she showed 'em that beautiful pair of tits she'd shoved into my face the day before.

Oh my God! The guys went crazy! They were like

a pack of hounds at feeding time, half of 'em grabbing and pulling so they could catch that little piece of cloth as it floated down, and the other half just lookin' at Teresa as she crammed her thumbs into her g-string and continued to dance and turn around the edge of the stage closest to me. It wasn't till she got right in front of me that I could see what had attracted her, because a guy with his back to me suddenly stood up and was waving a hundred dollar bill at her. I couldn't see who the guy was at first, but she saw him and began to do a special dance all for him right there on the edge of the stage. Nobody in the room really missed nothin', because she was as sexy on one side as she was on the other, but without her ever slowing down, those of us in front of her got an extra show as she near'bout pushed that guy's nose right into her snatch. And then, legal or not, just for him, she pulled aside that little g-string and showed him a clear glimpse of what he wanted to see most.

It was only a flash, but those of us at that end of the stage knew we'd been given a special treat, 'cause a second later, that g-string was back in its normal place and Teresa was up again and dancin' with the guy's hundred dollar bill stickin' out the front of it as Jesus's voice came over the loudspeaker announcing the final thirty seconds. Well, that announcement just seemed to set Teresa on fire. She'd done some pretty fancy stuff already, but in that final thirty seconds, she outdid herself. She bumped and she wiggled and she twirled and she stuck her thumbs in her g-string and twirled again while she teased that g-string down lower and lower until the exact final moment when, just like the night before, she jerked it down and the lights went out.

The audience went nuts, clapping their hands and shouting and whistling, but as the bright room lights flashed back on and Jesus was announcing that the Tiptop Club was closed for the night, I got a good look at the guy who'd stuck the hundred in Teresa's g-string, and I near'bout froze right there. It was Alphonso Ramirez, the man in snakeskin boots, and he was standing with his two buddies at the edge of the stage and clapping his hands like crazy.

Oh my God! For the first few seconds, I was almost paralyzed. In spite of all my planning and thinking and figuring about how I was gonna get him arrested, here he was less than ten feet in front of me and I was frozen in place thinking that now I was actually gonna have to do something. I had my pistol in my pocket, but I realized right away that the pistol wasn't gonna get me nowhere. I needed the police, but I'd left my cell phone in the truck, and that's where Officer Collins's number was. Oh, Jesus help me, I thought. I figured Ramirez wasn't gonna move very fast in that crowd, so I turned and ran back down the hall and out the back door to the truck where I grabbed the phone and ran back into the light where I could see what I was doin'. Luckily, I'd remembered to click off the door lock as I went out, so I got back inside easy enough, turned on the power, clicked the on button, and waited. It seemed like forever after I dialed before a sleepy woman's voice answered, and I realized I'd dialed Collins's home phone. "Let me speak to

Officer Collins," I said.

"Who is this? It's two o'clock in the morning," she said.

"It's Braxton Bragg. He told me to call him. I've got Ramirez in a corner."

"What?" she said, and I realized I wasn't makin' sense to her.

"Just let me talk to him," I said.

She said something, and then as I waited, I started moving back into the main part of the building because I realized I couldn't let Ramirez get out of sight. He was still standing there at the edge of the stage, but by now Jesus had come down out of the light booth and the two of them now were talkin' like old buddies. Officer Collins came on the line then, but in the noise I could hardly hear him, and at the same time, I realized that one of Ramirez's two sidekicks was lookin' directly at me holding the cell phone. I turned away and backed into the hall. "It's Braxton Bragg," I said to Officer Collins.

"Who?" he said, and I realized I was whispering. "Braxton Bragg," I said louder, "you know, the black guy from the clinic. I've got Ramirez spotted over here on Southside at the Tiptop Club."

"Now slow down," Collins said. "Tell me again."

And I could tell from the way he was talkin' that he hadn't been awake long. "OK," I said. "Listen. Remember a couple of days back...you were sitting in your car. I showed you the FBI poster for Alphonso Ramirez...the Mexican guy with five murders to his credit?"

"Oh, yeah."

"Well, he's over here at the Tiptop Club on South-side. I'm lookin' at him."

"Where are you now?"

"Where am I?"

"Yes."

"I'm inside the Tiptop Club. I'm standing in a doorway about ten feet behind him."

"Well, stay there. We're going to need you to identify him."

"This place is closing," I said. "He ain't gonna be here long."

"I'll get somebody on the way," Collins said. "Give me your number."

"I don't know my number. I just got this cell phone."

"Then call me back at...."

But I didn't let him finish because right then I looked up and here came Ramirez and Jesus and the two sidekicks walkin' down the hall right toward me. "Hold on," I said to Collins, "he's comin' this way." And I crammed the phone in my pocket and grabbed the vacuum cleaner like I was just gettin' started with my night's work.

"Braxton," Jesus said, "how's it going?" And he stopped and shook my hand in that friendly way I've noticed most Mexicans have when they meet somebody.

"Going fine," I told him, trying to be as friendly as I

could without having to look at Ramirez.

"This is my friend Ali Ramirez from my home town in Mexico," Jesus said. And like it or not, I found myself lookin' right into the eyes of Alphonso Ramirez and shakin' his hand. "Guess who he wants to see," Jesus said.

And of course, forgetting that Ramirez didn't speak much English, I tried to make a joke, "Yeah?" I said. "Has she got something he hasn't seen already?"

Of course, Jesus laughed at this, but Ramirez didn't even crack a smile till Jesus translated it into Spanish for him. "He says that sometimes we never see quite enough," Jesus said. And they walked on past me to the next door, which—from the star by the entrance—I figured was Teresa's dressing room.

I watched the four of them as I pulled my Hoover on toward the dining room, and then, as soon as Ramirez was safely inside Teresa's door, I pulled the phone back out of my pocket. "Collins, you still there?" I said.

"Yeah, I'm still here, but I was about to hang up. What's going on?"

I told him what had happened. "They're in Teresa's dressing room now," I said.

"Who's Teresa?"

"She's their lead dancer this week."

"OK," he said. "Can you stay where you are?"

"Yeah, I'm workin' down the hall from 'em."

"And you're sure it's Ramirez?"

"Yeah, I'm sure. I just shook hands with him."

"OK," he said again. "We've got cops from the city and the county on the way, along with a couple of federal guys. If he starts to go someplace else, call me on this number." And he started reelin' off this whole new telephone number.

"Wait," I said. "I ain't got nothin' to write it with."

"Then memorize it," he said. And he kept on givin' me numbers. I said 'em back to him out loud, trying to memorize 'em, but I knew I was shaky at best. "OK," I said. "I hope I've got it."

"Where are you going to be?"

"I'll be in the main dining room. I'll let you in through the front door."

"OK," he said, and then he was gone.

And of course, as soon as I heard his click, I remembered Ramirez's 9-millimeter pistol. "Holy shit!" I said to myself, "You must be nuts. You're puttin' yourself right in the line of fire!" But I didn't have more than half a minute to think about it, because right about then, I heard the door open, and here came the two sidekicks followed by Jesus and Ramirez with Teresa in between 'em. Teresa was wearing high heel shoes and a kind of mini skirt that showed off her legs real good, and Ramirez had his arm around her. And of course, he was lookin' at her and not payin' no mind to me at all, but this other guy in front of him was lookin' at me like he wanted me to just disappear.

"What's he doin' here?" he said to Jesus, and he was pointing right at me when he said it.

"He's cleaning up," Jesus told him.

"He's always hanging around," the guy said.

"He's just doing his work," Jesus said. "Come on." And he led the rest of 'em on past me toward the dining room. Now, of course, talk like that makes me nervous as hell, and I was happy to see 'em move on into the dining room. But my relief didn't last because Jesus turned right around and said, "Be sure to lock it up tight, Braxton." And I realized they were leaving before the cops got there.

"Yeah," I said, "I'll lock it up." But inside, I was thinkin', "God Almighty! What am I gonna do now?" I waited and tried to look cool as I watched my twenty thousand dollars walkin' out the door, but just as soon as they were all outside, I pulled the cell phone out of my pocket and tried to dial the number Collins gave me. By then, of course, I was so nervous I could hardly even hold the phone, much less dial, and when I did manage to dial, all I got were these little chimes and a sweet voice saying, "We're sorry, but your call cannot be completed as dialed."

"Holy shit!" I said. "They're gonna get away from me!" And I ran to the front door and looked out just in time to see Ramirez's big Lincoln backin' out of the parkin' place.

Well, that's when I really began to move. I don't think I've run so fast since I was on the high school track team—through the dining room and down the hall and out the back door to my truck. I'd dreamed about Ramirez and a chance at that twenty thousand dollars for too long to let him get away from me now, so I started the truck and eased around the corner of the building just as they pulled into the street. God! I was nervous! My truck has a stick shift, and every time I put my foot on the clutch, my whole leg wiggled up and down. I didn't have an idea in hell what I was gonna do if I ever got all of 'em cornered or if they got me cornered, but I wasn't gonna let a little thing like that stop me. This one was not gonna get away, if I could help it.

I could see 'em at a stop light about two blocks ahead, and I didn't want to get too close, so I pulled over to the curb and stopped and tried again to dial Collins's new number, but once again, all I got was the chimes and the sweet voice, and then I saw Ramirez pullin' away as the light turned green, and I gave up on the phone and started after him.

Fortunately, the road was pretty empty at 2:30 in the morning, so I was able to hang back and still keep the Continental in view without being seen. They were headin' straight west out Midlothian Turnpike past the shopping malls and the car dealerships and the furniture stores and the fast food places toward the country, and I kept 'em right in view until, without any warning at all, and still about a quarter of a mile ahead, they turned off and headed through this rabbit warren of a housing development and down a country road on the other side.

I guess my blood pressure must have shot up about fifty points then—first, because I didn't want to lose Ramirez and then because I knew that once we were off the straight highway, I would be a sitting duck if they had noticed me. I sped up toward the corner so I wouldn't lose 'em and tried to dial the phone again at the same time, which made me squeal my tires as I went around the turn, but this time, I just dialed 911 and had better luck.

"County emergency," the dispatcher said.

And I said, "Listen, I need police help."

"Where are you and what's the problem?" It was a woman's voice.

"I was just talkin' to Officer Collins from the Rich-mond police," I said. "I've got a fugitive spotted, and he was sending some cops to pick him up."

"Where are you?" the dispatcher said again, and I realized I didn't know where the hell I was.

"Listen," I said. "I'm somewhere out Midlothian Turnpike followin' these guys, but they just turned onto a side road."

"Which county are you in?"

"I don't know that either."

"Find a street sign," the dispatcher said. "I'll check with Richmond on another line."

"OK," I said. But about that time, just around a curve up ahead, I picked up the brake lights of the Continen-tal as the car slowed and turned into a dark driveway. "Hold on," I said, "they're turning in." For a minute, I wanted to stop behind 'em, but by then, I was so close, I knew I'd blow the whole thing if I didn't just keep goin'. So I sped on past that driveway and went on down the road about a half a mile before I pulled onto the shoulder. The dispatcher was still on the line, but by then, I could hear some strange sounds comin' through the phone.

"Sounds like your phone's getting weak," the dispatcher said.

"I reckon it is," I told her. "I'm somewhere on the back side of the moon. But I'm stopped now and I'm just past the place where these guys turned in."

"Wait," the dispatcher said, "what's your name?"

I told her.

"Officer Collins is looking for you at the Tiptop Club."

"Well, I ain't there."

"I'm going to try and patch you in to Collins," she said. I waited, and then I reached down and turned off my headlights so I wouldn't be so noticeable. It was a dark and totally empty country road with trees hanging over the roadway and leaves so thick I couldn't even see the stars. The only sounds I heard were these little squeaks and crackles that were comin' over the phone, until finally the dispatcher said, "Look, it's not working, but I've got Officer Collins on the other line. We've got to know where you are."

"OK," I said. "I'm gonna go look for a street sign or something. Tell him to come straight west on Midlothian Turnpike. But for God's sake, stay on the line."

"OK," the dispatcher said.

"Things are happening fast tonight."

"OK," she said again.

And then I made a U-turn and started back the way I'd come. At first I tried to make it with my lights off, but the night was so dark, I couldn't see squat without lights. So I turned 'em back on, and as I passed the driveway, I realized I could see the house numbers on the mailbox. "It's house number 13535," I told the dispatcher. "They're in 13535."

"OK," she said.

"Don't know the street yet, but that's the house."

"What're you driving?" the dispatcher said.

"I'm driving a red Toyota pickup," I told her. "Tell Collins to look for it." And then a couple of minutes later I saw I was comin' up to Midlothian Turnpike again, and I stopped. "Hold on," I said. "I'm at the Turnpike and I'm gonna get out and look for a street sign." I reached deep in my pocket and put my hand on my pistol and looked slowly around as I stepped out of the truck. There was absolutely nothin' moving on the highway, and the only sound I could hear was the hum of my engine and crunch of gravel under my shoes as I walked around the edge of the ditch with my flashlight hopin' there weren't no snakes crawlin' around where I couldn't see 'em. I looked first on one side and then on the other and then I walked all the way across the Turnpike, and that's where I found the street sign. Looked like somebody had run into it and knocked it down. "Here it is," I told the dispatcher as I pulled it up out of the weeds, "Here it is on the ground." But when she answered, she sounded so weak I could hardly hear her and my phone was makin' strange noises. "The name of the road is Knotting Hill," I said.

But she said, "What? I can't hear you."

And I was yellin' into the phone, "Knotting Hill! Knotting Hill!"

"Did you say, Rolling Hill?"

"No. Knotting Hill!" And then the phone gave a little crackle of static and went totally dead. "Oh Jesus help us!" I said. I tried to raise the dispatcher again, but when I looked down, I saw that the phone was so dead even the lights on the keypad had gone out. I looked up and down Midlothian Turnpike, and either way there was nothin' movin'. I looked down Knotting Hill Road, and it just disappeared into the blackness of the woods...no lights, no sign of life, no nothin'. And I tell you, I think then I felt about the loneliest I've ever felt in my life. "Braxton, why ain't you home in bed?" I said. "This is the craziest thing you've ever done in your whole fuckin' life—standing here at three o'clock in the morning on a dark country road, with the cops on one side and a bunch of killers on the other, and you can't see either one of 'em." I felt like runnin', like leaving the country, something. I just wanted to be shed of the whole damn business. Didn't want nothin' else to do with it. Didn't want to stay where I was, but didn't want to go back to the Tiptop Club or to the clinic or to the Museum or to ever clean another office building as long as I lived. I didn't even want to go back to Richmond.

But I couldn't stand at the intersection of a dark country road forever, either, so I propped the Knotting Hill

Road sign upright against the culvert in the ditch and stepped back in the truck. "Now what?" I said. Had the dispatcher ever heard the name of the road? I couldn't tell. I could stay there where I was at the corner and hope the cops would eventually come by and see me so I could lead them to the house where Ramirez was staying, and surely that seemed a reasonable thing to do. But at the same time, I knew there was no guarantee that the cops would ever get there or that Ramirez would still be at the house if they did. And if he slipped away, the whole deal would end up just another empty click!—like that shotgun shell that wouldn't go off when I was a kid, Click!—just another case of 'come back tomorrow' or 'don't call us, we'll call you.' And I put the truck in gear and turned around. "No sir," I said out loud, "not this time. That son of a bitch is not gonna walk away from me." And I headed back down that dark country road.

15

About a hundred yards before I got to the driveway, I pulled off the road and onto the shoulder. From there, through the trees at the end of the driveway, I could see the house lights—the only lights for miles around—and I figured Ramirez and Teresa and the rest of 'em were up to sump'n I could only guess at. I wasn't about to go down there by myself to find out what it was, you understand, but at least from that spot on the road I could see who came and went. So I cut off the engine and cut out the lights and just waited in the dark, hopin' the police would find me sooner or later. That was when the whole day began to get to me. Suddenly, I was tired, tired as I'd ever been. "Don't you let your ass go to sleep," I said to myself, "because you will be buyin' the farm, if you do."

I blinked my eyes and rubbed my face and rolled down the windows so I could get plenty of air, and then I realized I needed to take a leak. So I got out and went over to the edge of the woods, but—like always happens when you're tryin' to sneak a quick piss on the side of the road—no sooner did I get started than here came a car around the curve. Oh shit! I tried to quit pissin', but it took longer than I thought and I didn't want to be seen, so even before I was able to stop, I plunged into the woods and hid down among the weeds and briars and succeeded in wetting my pants pretty good in the process. God Almighty, I hated doing that! But it was the right thing to do, because whoever it was in the car stopped beside my truck and some guy got out and looked at it. He opened the driver's door and looked inside and said somethin' I couldn't make out, and then he got back inside the car and they drove on to the driveway and turned in toward the house. "OK," I said to myself, "this is gettin' bigger by the minute."

I stayed in the woods for a while after that, but in spite of my wet pants, I figured that sittin' in the truck would still be better than sittin' in the woods with the red bugs and snakes, so I stumbled out the thicket and was getting ready to get back in the truck when I looked up and here came three more cars in a row comin' around the curve. This time there was no chance of hiding, so I just stood there by the driver's door rather than run, and you can guess my relief when I saw the brace of lights on top of that first car. On man! Seeing them police cars was like seeing the sunrise after a dark night. I waved 'em down, and Collins got out of the first car and came over. "What've you got for us," he said.

I told him who was at the house—at least the ones I knew. "But two more just drove in about five minutes ago," I said. "And Ramirez is the only one I really know anything about."

"OK," Collins said. "But you wait here because we're going to need you to help identify these people."

"Right," I said. And then he told the rest of the police what I'd told him, and they moved on up the road where
they parked one cruiser in the driveway and then walked on
down to the house in the dark.

Now I can't say for sure what actually happened
down at that farmhouse, but the night was so calm and still,
I could hear some of it through the open windows of the
pickup. I heard dogs barkin', and I heard the police knockin'
on the door, and then I heard somebody shout, "Police! Police! Stop where you are!" and then there was this shouting
and noises like somebody was runnin', and then everything
was quiet—with me straining to hear every little sound until
a couple of minutes later I heard this crashin' through the
brush, and I saw this shadow come bustin' out of the woods,
and before I could even blink, somebody was jerkin' open
the passenger door and crawlin' into my truck with a pistol
in his hand and shoutin' at me in Spanish somethin' like,
"Drive! Hijo de puta! Drive!" And I knew I was face to face
with Ramirez himself.

Now, there ain't no way in hell to plan what you
might do if somebody jerks open your car door and crawls
into the seat beside you. I sure didn't have no plan. I just
reacted, and what I did was hit the latch on my door and
roll into the dark, rollin' out of the driver's door as fast as
Ramirez crawled into the passenger door. Goddamn! I hit
the running board with my head and fell face down on the
gravel outside and kept on rollin' while I tried to get up, and
then Ramirez fired his pistol after me. Oh, Jesus! Don't

ever let anybody tell you that gettin' shot don't hurt much. People in the movies that act all big and brave after bein' shot...well, it's bullshit. That bullet hit my left shoulder, and I tell you I never had nothin' in my life hurt me as much as that thing did. I mean, it knocks your breath out, makes you feel like you just don't want to move again. But that night I knew I had to move because I knew Ramirez would kill me if I didn't. So I rolled to my knees and hid around behind the tailgate as I heard Ramirez stomping on the floorboard and swearin' because he couldn't find the key. You see, when I went to relieve myself earlier, I'd pulled the key out of the ignition and I had it in my pocket. But I figured it won't gonna take Ramirez more than a second to figure that out and come lookin' for me.

Well, this is where my earlier planning began to kick in. Remember that ever since I'd found out that Ramirez was a killer with a price on his head, I had started to imagine every possible situation that might come up for me to get him caught. My favorite was just finding him in a restaurant where the police could walk in and arrest him without incident. But I knew there were a million other things that could happen as well, and day after day, riding along in my truck, I had imagined one scenario after another. I had imagined him in a parking lot where I was lookin' for him as he dodged between cars; I had imagined him in an abandoned building; I had pictured him in a high speed car chase down the highway; I had seen him turning the tables and coming to get me in an office building late at night, with him creeping along one wall and me waiting around the corner along another wall. And that was the picture that clicked in now. It wasn't in an office building, but still, I could hear him gettin' out of the driver's door and walkin' back along the side of the truck toward me. We were about to meet at the corner of the tailgate, just like at the corner of a wall in the office building I had imagined, and I had to be ready for him. So in spite of the pain in my shoulder, I crouched low in the shadow behind the tailgate and waited, and as quietly as I could, I pulled my little .32 Walthur out of my pocket. Of course, I'd been out there in the dark a lot longer than he had, and my eyes had adjusted pretty good. So I just waited while he took one step and then another right along the side of the truck until I could see him clearly no more than an arm's length away when I reached out and stuck my pistol in his ear and said, "Freeze, mutha fucker!" And he did it.

Oh My God! He did it! 'Course, if he hadn't done it, mad as I was about bein' shot, I would have truly blown him a new ear hole right there. But he did it. "On the ground," I said to him. "Drop the gun and get on your knees on the ground." He sort of resisted then, and if I'd been able to trust my left arm I'd have tripped him and thrown him on the ground right there. But I was in no mood to fuck around, so I just rotated my pistol slightly to the side and fired it toward the sky about two inches away from his ear. And that's when I tripped him. Kicked his feet right out from under him. "On the ground!" I shouted at him. "Get your ass on the ground!" And no sooner was he there than I was on his back with my pistol again in his right ear. "OK, mutha fucker! Don't move," I said. And it was about then that I heard the police comin' out of the woods beside the truck. They had lights and they had radios and somebody in the bunch had a flash camera, and they were shouting at me to put the gun down and back away, but I don't remember doin' any of it because right about then, I guess I passed out.

16

After that, my memories for the next twenty-four hours are all jumbled. I've got one memory of wakin' up in an ambulance with a medic workin' on my left arm. "What happened?" I said to the medic. "Did they get Ramirez?"

And he said, "Yeah. I think they did. And you lost a lot of blood while they were at it."

"What about my truck?" I said. "Where's my truck?"

"I don't know for sure," he said. "But they probably brought it in." And then the next thing I remember, I woke up at the Medical College. Must have been a whole day later, but the first thing I saw was Sadie standin' at the foot of the bed, and I swear, I never saw nothin' so pretty in all my life. She was talkin' to the doctor, and she sounded like she was really tore up about what had happened to me. I said sump'n to her, and she broke off what she was sayin' to the doctor and came over to me and just hugged me right there in the bed. "Oh, Braxton," she said, "I thought we had lost you."

"Naw, Baby, you ain't lost me," I said. "I'm gonna be around to give you trouble for a while longer." And I saw she actually had tears in her eyes—which is a thing I hadn't seen in a long time, if I'd ever seen it. I guess when people live together for years and both of 'em are workin' like hell just tryin' to scratch up a livin', they get so used to each other they start actin' more like business partners or roommates rather than husbands or wives, and they kind of forget why they're together in the first place. It takes something like gettin' shot to make 'em really remember it.

The doctor came over about then and told me he'd had a big job trying to tie all my bones and muscles and tendons back together but that he thought my arm was gonna be in pretty good shape and that I could go home the next day. So I thanked him for that, and then as the doctor left the room, Sadie said, "You realize you're famous, don't you?" And I said, no, I didn't realize that. But she reached up and pulled a newspaper out from under her purse on the bedside table and held it up in front of me. "You made the front page," she said. And there, sure enough, smack dab in the middle of the front page was a picture of me sittin' on Ramirez's back with my pistol in his ear. "You captured one of the ten most wanted men in the United States," she said. And then she read me part of the article that went along with the picture. Seems that a police reporter had been ridin' with the cops that night and was there to snap the photo when they busted out of the woods on Ramirez and me. "Everybody's talking about it," Sadie said. "The phone started ringing early this morning." And then she read some more of the article, which included a note about me bein' in line to receive the twenty thousand dollar reward. "That's just wonderful!" she said. "Twenty thousand dollars! Braxton, that's just unbelievable!"

"Um humn. We'll see what we'll see, won't we?" I said.

But we didn't have long to wait before interesting things started to happen. Even before the morning was out, my brother Billy came in to see me, and not long after that, here came my cousin Frank—the one, if you remember, who was so rude to me in his law office the day I went to check on the laws about carrying a pistol. But on this day, Frank was just as nice and polite as he could be. And while he was still there in the hospital room, in walked his brother, my cousin Clarence, the one I said was so uppity he didn't want 'to know no more niggers.' And he was the same way. Couldn't say enough nice things.

"Good job!" he said, "Good job! Braxton, you're a brave man to do all that."

"A little fame and fortune sure does a lot to improve a man's social status, don't it?" I said. And they just laughed, but I think they got my meaning.

Anyway, I thanked 'em for coming by. But Sadie, of course, didn't miss a thing. She was cluckin' her tongue like my mama used to do the minute they were out the door. "Braxton, there'e no point in being ugly to those boys," she said.

"No, I suppose not," I told her. "Surely I'd rather have peace than otherwise. But, Sadie, I can't help remembering that a week ago, they wouldn't have had time for me to even sit down in their offices."

"They just don't know better," she said.

"No, I guess not," I said. "But tell me what's changed." And without waiting for her to speak, I went on. "Ain't nothin' changed. Really. I'm the same nigger I was last week. But now, I've had my picture in the paper and I've got the hope of gettin' a little money. So that makes me somebody worth knowing, right?"

"Oh, Braxton, that's the way the world is."

"Yeah," I said. "I guess it is. But I don't have to like it." And then I laughed. "But I am glad they came by."

One of the best things that happened that day was the visit from the US marshal, a man named Franklin. He came in and shook hands and made me feel really good because he said that not only was Texas panting to get Ramirez back for what he'd done down there, but that catching him was also going to clear up a lot of criminal cases here in Richmond.

Well, of course, I was glad that whatever I'd done had made the town better, but after a few minutes of him praising my selfless public spirit and all, there seemed to be one thing left hanging, and since he didn't mention it before he started out, I just had to butt in and stop him. "What about the reward?" I said. This of course, embarrassed Sadie, who is far more kind and public spirited than I ever was, and it seemed like it embarrassed the marshal, too. "The 'Wanted' poster, offered a reward of $20,000," I said. "When do you think I might get that?"

"Well, I'm just not authorized to talk about that," he said. "A lot of the time, they'll have a little ceremony down-town to show our appreciation. But I'll check into it and get back with you."

"Yes. I'd appreciate it," I told him. And I pointed to my arm. "As you can see, I'm gonna have a few public spirited expenses to take care of."

"Right," Mr. Bragg," he said. "Right. I'll be in touch."

"You don't think they'd really go back on their offer of the reward, do you?" Sadie said after he was gone.

And I just looked at her. "What was that you said earlier about the way the world is?" I said. "People's memories are mighty short, Sadie. But we're gonna keep reminding them."

Well, I went home the next afternoon like the doctor had told me, and we heard the telephone ringing even before we had opened the front door. Sadie hurried on in to answer it, and then she handed it to me. "It's Lucy Shields," she said.

And I tell you, Lucy was fit to be tied, bubbling along like a hot Coca-Cola in July. "Braxton, you are the bravest man I ever knew in all my life," she said.

"I was in the right place at the right time," I told her.

"That may be," she said, "but our great great-grand-daddy would be mighty proud of you bringing that cold-blooded killer to justice."

"I'm glad you approve."

"Approve! I think it's just marvelous. And I want you to know everybody at the church thinks it's marvelous, too. They're going to offer you the job of sexton."

"Really?"

"Yes, if you still want it."

Well, I had to sit down on that one. I'd already given up the idea of that job, and now I hardly knew what to say. "That's quite a surprise," I said finally. "Of course, I won't be able to start for a while on account of my hurt shoulder."

"Oh, that's all right," Lucy said. "I don't think anybody would mind about that. But Braxton, listen, I think they might even offer you more money if you were to ask for it."

"I never was very good at doing that," I said. "I sort of leave it up to the man that's payin' the bills. But if you could mention it to 'em for me...."

"Just leave it to me," Lucy said. "Leave it to me."

"Yeah, I'd appreciate it," I said. And then I hung up and sat back and looked at Sadie. "They want me to take the job at the church," I said. "Do you know what that means?"

"Well, for one thing, it means you're going to get retirement and health insurance," she said.

"Yeah, that's right, but, Sadie, more important than that, it means I can quit the job at the clinic," I said. "I don't need to go back down there and have people curse at me and try to burn me up. I don't have to go back and stumble around in the dark and step on another bag of fetuses that somebody left layin' around. I can tell them people they need to get their act together."

"That's mighty good," she said. "Certainly seems

like the right thing to do."

"I might even be able to quit the Corporation."

She looked at me for a second and nodded and then walked over to the closet to hang up her coat, walkin' slow like there was something heavy on her mind. "You don't want to give up too much," she said. "But tell me this...while you're giving up things...." She leaned back against the closet door and looked at me in that way she's got that tells you she knows every secret in your life. "The newspaper said you first spotted Ramirez at the Tiptop Club," she said. And suddenly, I could feel this cold chill like ice water pouring down the back of my neck. But she went on. "I thought that was one of the most interesting things in that story," she said. "Tell me about the Tiptop Club, Braxton. Tell me about the Tiptop Club."

Printed in the United States
112635LV00002B/45/A